ON the day that Giles Bradwell came again to the Dower House, Imelda was returning from an errand to one of the neighboring farms. At the first sound of approaching hoof-beats she felt a flicker of apprehension, and cast a quick glance over her shoulder, but one glimpse of the familiar chestnut horse and tall, scarlet-coated rider allayed her momentary alarm, replacing it with a rush of gladness and excitement which took her unawares. She stopped and waited for him with flushed cheeks and shining eyes, and, when he dismounted beside her, stretched out her hand to him in an unselfconscious gesture of welcome.

He took the slight fingers and kissed them as though he would have preferred to kiss her lips, and then for a few moments they stood handfasted, just looking at each other in a silence that somehow said things they did not yet dare to put into words. When at last they spoke, it was to be in polite and formal phrases that had nothing whatsoever to do with what their eyes had been soundlessly saying.

Fawcett Crest Books
by Sylvia Thorpe:

A FLASH
OF SCARLET

Sylvia Thorpe

A FAWCETT CREST BOOK • NEW YORK

A FLASH OF SCARLET

Published by Fawcett Crest Books, CBS Publications, the Consumer Publishing Division of CBS Inc., by arrangement with the Hutchinson Publishing Group.

ISBN: 0-449-23533-5

Printed in the United States of America

10 9 8 7 6 5 4 3 2 1

A FLASH
OF SCARLET

Part 1

Imelda was weeping and terrified, but neither her terror nor her tears had any effect upon the two youths, both far gone in drink, who held her prisoner between them on the rough wooden bench. They had been already halfway to drunkenness when they first invaded the little isolated ale-house where Imelda and her servant, utterly lost and overtaken by nightfall and heavy rain, had sought shelter, and they had been drinking steadily ever since.

They had come swaggering into the long, low-pitched room which was kitchen and tap-room in one, shaking the rain from sodden cloaks and plumed hats, cursing the weather and the ill-luck which had forced them to halt here instead of at some comfortable inn where good wine and good entertainment might be had. In hectoring tones they commanded the old tavern-keeper to fetch them the best he had of food and drink, and then one of them caught sight of Imelda, shrinking a little in a corner of the settle by the fire, and his eyes brightened.

"Why, what's here? We're to have fair company tonight, if naught else." He swept her a bow that caused him to stagger a little. "God save you, mistress! Are you benighted, like ourselves, by this pestilent weather?"

"Would she be here else?" His companion shouldered him aside and stood grinning down at her. "Fair flowers don't bloom on middens." Without shifting his gaze from Imelda, he snapped his fingers at the tavern-keeper. "Bring wine for the lady, too. She'll drink with us."

With a murmur of protest Imelda shook her head. Her servant, Jedediah, watchful in the background, moved stolidly forward to stand between her and the two young men.

"Good sirs, my mistress has already supped. We have been travelling all day, and she is weary."

For the moment that gave them pause. Jedediah's hair might be grey, but his stocky, powerful build and resolute air left no doubt of either his ability or his willingness to protect his charge. That was why he, of her family's few remaining servants, had been chosen to escort Imelda Hallett on the long journey from her home to her kinsman's house. The young man shrugged ill-humouredly and went to throw himself down on one of the benches flanking the bare, drink-stained table in the middle of the room, and after another lingering look at Imelda his companion followed suit.

Imelda breathed a sigh of relief, but she was to find that she had rejoiced too soon. For a time the newcomers paid no more heed to her, being occupied with the indifferent wine and scanty fare which was all that the meagre resources of the house could provide, but neither their behaviour nor their conversation was reassuring, the tone of the latter growing steadily coarser as the wine sank lower in the bottle. She would have liked to withdraw, but though the tavern-keeper and his wife had reluctantly agreed to provide her with a bed for the night, she had no idea where this might be and was unwilling to attract attention to herself by asking.

With mounting uneasiness she watched her fellow-guests consume a second bottle of wine and call for a third, and knew that her disquiet was shared by Jedediah and even by the old couple, whose satisfaction at the unwonted trade was obviously tempered by misgivings regarding the possible results of such heavy drinking. It was now quite dark, and the rain continued to drum on the roof and stream down the tiny, deep-set windows in an unrelenting downpour.

The elder of the two at the table set down an empty glass, stretched, belched and cast a somewhat hazy glance around the room. It settled on Imelda, lingering in a meaning fashion that brought a flush to her cheeks, and then he heaved himself up and moved unsteadily towards her.

"Curst unfriendly, aren't you, my pretty?" he said thickly. "What ails you that you sit moping here 'stead of joining our honest merry-making? Come, now—!"

He broke off, for Jedediah had once more interposed his solid person between him and Imelda. The youth swore at him and tried to shoulder him aside, and next moment received a shove in the chest that sent him staggering back to sprawl against the table, half on and half off the bench from which he had lately risen.

He struggled up, his face crimson with fury and a dangerous glitter in his eyes, and launched himself at the servant as his companion came stumbling round the table to his aid. The fight was short-lived, for though Jedediah put up a spirited resistance he could not defend himself against two attackers at once, and when the younger of them swung a savage blow to the back of his head with an empty bottle he dropped where he stood, and lay prone and motionless, with a trickle of blood soaking into his hair.

Imelda screamed and flung herself on her knees beside him, but the larger youth seized her by the shoulders and jerked her to her feet again, while his fellow stood swaying slightly and regarding the result of his handiwork with a fatuous, satisfied grin. Imelda's captor guffawed.

"Shrewdly done, Jack! Interfering jackanapes is well served. Be still, you little vixen!" he added to his struggling prisoner. "I'll teach you friendlier ways than this before the night's past."

He shifted his hold on her, so that his arms were round her, pinning her own arms to her sides and holding her fast, her back against his chest. He bent his head, and she cried out with fright and anger as she felt his lips against her neck. Jack tossed the broken bottle aside and advanced, grinning.

"Rob you, Luke! Will you keep all the sport to yourself? What of my reward for ridding us of the servant?"

"Aye, you've earned it." Luke released Imelda with a slight push that sent her stumbling into Jack's ready arms, and dropped down again on the bench. Chuckling, he slopped wine into a glass and then reached up to jerk the sobbing girl down beside him so abruptly that Jack, taken unawares, flopped down also. Luke thrust the glass against Imelda's lips.

"You'll drink with me, sweeting, like it or not," he told her, laughing. "Should have done so at first asking, but better late than not at all."

She resisted frantically, but though most of the wine was spilt, splashing impartially over both of them, she was forced, choking and gasping, to swallow a portion of it. He laughed again, threw the empty glass aside and bent her backwards across his knees, kissing her brutally while she sobbed and writhed in his arms.

The old tavern-keeper, ashen-faced, was moved to timorous protest. "Good sirs, I pray you, let the lady be. 'Tis shame to—!"

"Cease cackling, you old fool! Who gave you leave to spoil sport?" Jack came to his feet again and dealt the old fellow a buffet that sent him sprawling, to the accompaniment of a shrill scream from his wife. "Mend your manners, or you'll be served the same as that crow's meat yonder."

He turned back to his companion, eyed them with disfavour and then gripped Luke by the shoulder and wrenched him away from the girl, saying in an aggrieved tone:

"Od rot it! Am I to have all the pains and you all the pleasure? May I be damned if I take second place to you!"

"You'll be damned if you don't!" Luke glared furiously up at his erstwhile crony, but Jack, drunk now as much with triumph as with wine, grabbed their victim and tried to drag her away by main force. Luke, retaining his hold on her, sought with equal vigour to prevent him, and Imelda screamed, as much with the hurt of this rough handling as with fear.

The tavern door swung open, so that the flames of the candles flickered wildly and then steadied as it was slammed shut again, while the occupants of the room froze into stillness and stared at the man who had entered. To Imelda's panic-stricken eyes he seemed a veritable giant, for his head in the gleaming, dripping steel helmet brushed the ceiling, while the breadth of him, in the heavy, shrouding cloak, gave the impression of filling the room. Just for an instant he stood as motionless as they, and then in two strides he was beside them, and there was a flash of steel and scarlet beneath the sodden, mud-spattered cloak as he seized Jack, who was the nearest, by the scruff of the neck and hurled him contemptuously aside.

Luke cursed hoarsely and groped for his sword, but before his fingers reached the hilt he was dealt a blow which lifted him clean off his feet and dropped him, senseless, a yard away. Imelda, with the room swaying madly around her, felt a strong, supporting hand in a wet leather gauntlet gripping her elbow, and looked up—far up—into a stern, square-jawed young face and cool, blue-grey eyes. He guided her to a seat, but at once turned from her to the old woman, already launched upon a shrill-voiced account of the outrages committed by the two unwelcome guests.

Imelda felt a little spurt of resentment at this indifference, but a moment later, realizing that her bodice was ripped open and her bosom bare, was thankful for his tact in not looking at her again. With trembling fingers she sought to restore some decency to her apparel, while the tavern-keeper, with one side of his face already beginning to swell and darken, added his complaints to his wife's, until the newcomer's voice broke calmly in upon their almost incoherent gabbling.

"Has your cellar a stout door that can be barred?"

It was a deep voice, and quiet, yet with an underlying note of authority which won from the tavern-keeper a prompt, if somewhat bewildered assent. Imelda's rescuer went on:

"Then it will be an apt place to bestow these two louts until morning." He turned to Jack, who had picked himself up and was now sitting on the far side of the table with his head resting on his hands. "Bestir yourself, and bring your comrade with you. And should you be tempted to sample the contents of your prison, be warned that a strict accounting will be demanded before you leave this place."

Partially sobered by what had happened, and thoroughly cowed, Jack did as he was told, though the stranger was obliged to help him haul Luke to his feet and drag him off to the cellar. Imelda, having restored some order to her appearance, forced her trembling limbs up from her seat and went to kneel beside Jedediah. The old woman, rocking to and fro on a nearby stool with her skinny arms clutched across her middle, said dolefully:

"He be hurt mortal bad, poor soul. Mortal bad."

Imelda feared that she was right. Jedediah had not moved, and his grey hair was now dark and sticky with blood. She tried to turn him on his back, but he was a heavy man and she was still shaking too much herself to exert a great deal of strength.

A shadow fell across her; the deep voice said: "By your leave, madam," and she drew back a little as the stranger dropped to one knee at her side. Sitting back on her heels, she watched anxiously as he examined the unconscious man, and then lifted him and laid him on the settle, telling the old woman to dress the wound.

"I will tend him myself," Imelda said quickly, then, lest this sounded ungracious, added in explanation: "He is an old and loyal servant, and was injured trying to protect me."

"As you wish," he agreed indifferently, and moved away, nodding to the old woman, who hobbled off to fetch what was necessary.

Imelda bent anxiously over Jedediah, loosening the clothing about his neck and laying a hand on his forehead, but wondering all the while how adequately to word the thanks which she knew she owed to the providential newcomer. How *did* one thank a strange young man—especially when he seemed so aloof and uncaring—for saving one from being brutally ravished?

Still uncertain what to say, but knowing that something must be said, she turned to face him, and was at once aware of an inward, instinctive recoiling. He had discarded his cloak, so that the scarlet and steel she had previously only glimpsed was now fully revealed, and though she had recognized him for what he was the moment she set eyes on him, she could not now subdue her innate antagonism. Hard though it had seemed before to express her thanks, she found it infinitely harder to acknowledge a debt of gratitude to a man who stood before her in the heated uniform of Cromwell's New Model Army.

Though he betrayed no sign of it, Giles Bradwell observed the girl's involuntary stiffening at sight of his uniform, and reflected exasperatedly that this was of a piece with the ill-luck which had dogged him all day, that he should be obliged to rescue a lady in distress, and that she should be a Royalist. He had seen that look too often to mistake it now. The Civil Wars were over, but the Ironside army, under Cromwell, was the master of England, and old enmities survived.

"I have to thank you, sir, for coming to my aid," she said after a moment, in a voice as stiff as her bearing. "Had you not come when you did—!"

"No thanks are needful," he interrupted. "Chance alone brought me here, but I am glad of it."

It was not what he had intended to say. He had spoken hastily to spare them both embarrassment, but had failed in his purpose. An uncomfortable silence fell, and they were both glad when the woman returned with a bowl of water and some rags for bandages.

Imelda busied herself with her injured servant, and
Giles sat down at the table and looked resignedly at
the very frugal fare the tavern-keeper set before him.
He had been in the saddle all day; he was wet and
cold and hungry, and would have preferred to eat
the inadequate meal and then stretch himself out by
the fire and sleep, but he supposed courtesy demanded
that he should inquire of the girl how she came to be
in her present plight, and offer any assistance that lay
in his power. The servant, from the look of him,
would be of little use to her for some time to come.

When Imelda, with some help from the woman of
the house, had done all she could for Jedediah, she
pulled a stool close to the settle and sat down, anxiously studying the servant's pallid face. He had re-
gained a measure of consciousness but seemed unaware
of her presence, or of his surroundings, and fear
clawed at her again as she contemplated the immediate
future. She had no idea where they were or how far
from their destination—their inquiries had been met
with blank stares from the old couple—or how, without Jedediah to depend on, she was to cope with the
rest of the journey. This was the first time in her life
that she had travelled more than a dozen miles from
home.

She stole a covert glance at the silent man at the
table, for, enemy though he was, he might well prove
to be her only source of advice and assistance. He had
laid aside the helmet, and without it looked younger
and a little less forbidding, for his hair, cropped just
below the level of his ears, was fair and very thick,
and, now that the rain was drying out of it, showed a

disarming tendency to curl. Though not quite the avenging giant he had seemed to her at first, he was certainly very tall, with a splendid breadth of shoulder and length of limb which were emphasized by the severity of that objectionable uniform. Even in her present anxiety and distress, Imelda was feminine enough to appreciate that he was an exceedingly personable young man.

Unexpectedly he looked towards her, and she flushed scarlet, furious that he should have caught her watching him, and more furious still that the aloof gaze should hold hers so effortlessly. After a moment he said abruptly:

"Had you far to travel, madam, when this vile weather forced you to halt here?"

"I cannot tell, for we had lost our way long before, and the people here cannot help us. We are bound for a village called Conyngton St. John."

"Whence have you come?"

"From my home in Wiltshire. We lay last night at Exeter."

His brows lifted. "You must have been wandering in circles then. Conyngton St. John is barely half a day's journey from here."

Her eyes brightened. "Do you know the place, sir?"

"I know where it lies. I am bound for Plymouth and can guide you, if you wish, to within a couple of miles of the village."

"We shall be grateful, sir, if you will." A shadow crossed her face, and she looked again at her servant. "If Jedediah is well enough to ride."

Giles thought this extremely unlikely, but kept the

reflection to himself. Studying Imelda with a faint frown, he said, "Have you kinfolk in Conyngton St. John?"

She nodded. "Yes. The squire, Sir Darrell Conyngton, is my cousin and I am to be waiting gentlewoman to his wife." She hesitated, wondering if this had given the Roundhead too grand an impression, for Sir Darrell was a noted Royalist. After a moment she added, with a defensive note in her voice of which she was unaware: "Of course, I shall have numerous other duties as well, for my kinsman's household is not large."

Giles accepted this without comment. The name of Conyngton had struck a faint chord of memory; something he had heard in Plymouth of the great losses the man had sustained during the wars. Yet it seemed that there was a branch of the family more impoverished still, if this girl was going as some sort of upper servant to Conyngton's wife. Dowerless, no doubt, poor wench, Giles reflected with fleeting pity, and her parents glad enough, as like as not, for their kinsman to house and feed her in return for service. He thought for a moment of his own young sister at home in Bristol, with the security of their father's ample fortune around her, and contrasted her probable future with that of the shabby girl crouching on her stool beside the unconscious serving-man. A bleak enough prospect, hers, as a poor relation in her cousin's house; he was glad he had arrived on the scene in time to save her from the shameful ordeal which had threatened her tonight.

Jedediah stirred and moaned, and she bent forward

eagerly, but though his eyes were half open he did not seem to see her, and only muttered something incoherent, rolling his bandaged head from side to side. She straightened up and turned a frightened face towards Giles again.

"He does not know me," she said in a low, unsteady voice. "If only I had some remedy, something which would give him ease, but the woman here seems to have no stores of medicines."

Giles got up and went to bend over the injured man, studying him narrowly. After a few moments he straightened up again and shook his head.

"There is little that you or anyone can do for him at present," he said kindly. "He has not yet recovered his senses, and so I doubt whether he is in any pain. It would be wise to take some rest yourself against tomorrow's needs." She looked mistrustfully at him and he added in a reassuring tone: "No, I am not a surgeon, but I have seen many wounded men and you may take my word that it is so. Can these people furnish you with a bed?"

She nodded. He stopped again to set a hand beneath her elbow, compelling her to rise, at the same time saying authoritatively over his shoulder to the tavern-keeper:

"The lady is weary. Have your wife show her where she may rest."

Imelda felt vaguely that she ought to protest, but she was overwhelmed by the size of him towering beside her, by that hated uniform, by his calm assumption that he would be obeyed. Though she did not realize it, she was almost light-headed from exhaustion and shock, and the thought of protesting took no root in her will. When the old woman came hobbling up to them she followed her without a word.

Tired though she was, Imelda passed a wretched night, for which the discomfort of her quarters was only partly to blame. Giles Bradwell's estimate of her situation had come close to the truth, for the Hallett family was now very poor. They had never been rich, and sixteen years before her elder brother, Nicholas, had counted himself fortunate when his wealthy kinsman, Sir Darrell Conyngton, father of the present baronet, had invited him to become steward of his large estate; but Nicholas, following his benefactor to war under the standard of King Charles, had died at the battle of Newbury. Two other brothers had fallen in the same doomed cause, and the family's modest substance diminished almost to nothing under the demands of war, and later of the savage fines and taxes imposed by the victorious Parliament. What little was left must be husbanded for the one surviving son and his children, and there were no marriage-portions for Imelda and her three sisters. At last, reluctantly, but not knowing where else to turn, their father had written to Sir Darrell. . . .

The squire of Conyngton St. John had suffered like the rest, but compared to the Halletts he was still prosperous. In reply to his kinsman's plea for help had come the offer to take one of the girls into his household; his wife, with a young and growing family, would be glad of a companion and waiting-gentlewoman; he left it to Mr. Hallett to decide which of his daughters it should be.

The choice had fallen upon the youngest, nineteen-year-old Imelda. Her wishes had not been consulted. In that year of 1655 a father's word was law, especially where daughters were concerned, and children were not expected to question decisions made on their behalf. Not that Imelda had tried to do so. There was little for her to look forward to as the youngest of four spinster daughters in an impoverished household, and though her heart misgave her at the prospect of leaving everything familiar and going far away to make her home among strangers, there was at the back of her mind a tiny, unacknowledged thought that any change must be for the better. At home she could see the future stretching straight before her, empty and unrewarding, but the move to her cousin's house at least offered a bend in the road, a possibility that life had something more to offer.

That thought had buoyed her up throughout the preparations for her journey, and enabled her to take leave of her family with some degree of composure, but jogging along behind Jedediah, pillion on the old grey double-gelding, with her few meagre possessions in the saddle-bags, she had had plenty of time to wonder what lay ahead of her. She knew nothing of the Conyngtons, save that they were still young, and her ladyship Sir Darrell's second wife. Apprehension had grown until it overshadowed all else, and she had set out on the third, and what should have been the last, day of her journey in a mood of the deepest foreboding.

Now these fears were reinforced by others more immediate. If Jedediah were not well enough to travel in the morning she had no idea how they were ever to reach Conyngton St. John, for though the Roundhead officer had offered to guide them, she could not expect him to wait upon her convenience. He would go about whatever business was awaiting him in Plymouth, and she would be thrown entirely upon her own resources. The dismay which flooded over her at that thought brought humiliating realization of the degree to which she was depending on help from one whom she ought to regard as an enemy, and, rolling over on her uncomfortable couch, Imelda finally gave way to tears.

It was little wonder that morning found her pale and heavy-eyed. Towards dawn she had fallen into an exhausted sleep, and it was broad daylight when she woke, her head throbbing and her whole body stiff and aching from the bruises she had suffered the evening before, and from the hardness of her bed. Dragging herself up, she scrambled down the steep ladder to the room below, where to her immense relief she found that Jedediah was now in full possession of his senses, though it was painfully obvious that he was in no case to travel.

"But you must go on, Miss Imelda," he told her weakly. "The Major—Giles Bradwell, his name is— says he'll take you to Conyngton St. John. 'Tis but a mile or two out of his way."

"Jedediah, I cannot leave you here alone! You are ill. You need proper care."

"I shall do well enough, mistress, but it's not fitting

for you to stay in such a place as this. After what happened last night I'll not rest easy till you are safe at Sir Darrell's house. It sits ill with me to see you go with a stranger, but needs must." He closed his eyes, and a spasm of pain contracted his face. "Needs must!"

Imelda glanced about her; Bradwell was nowhere to be seen. "I would rather stay with you," she whispered. "Perhaps by tomorrow—!"

He shook his head, and groaned. "Nay and even so, who then could show us the way? Do you fear to travel with him? I think you need not, Roundhead though he be."

Imelda thought about this. No, she was not afraid to travel with Major Bradwell, for she felt instinctively that he was to be trusted. Perhaps, she reflected with a flicker of rueful humour, she thought so because he had regarded her with such utter indifference the night before.

This led inevitably to consideration of her present appearance, and the need to remedy it. Her saddle-bags were still in the corner where Jedediah had placed them when they arrived. She found her comb, and the little pewter-framed mirror which had been her mother's parting gift, and, having refreshed herself by bathing her hands and face with cold water grudgingly provided by the old woman, she took the pins from her hair and let it down.

Imelda was proud of her hair. Rich brown in colour, falling in thick waves to below her waist and clustering in natural curls on each side of her face, it was her one real claim to beauty. For the rest, her eyes were brown, too, and handsome enough, but deep-set beneath straight, rather thick brows; her face was thin; her complexion resembled more the dusky gold of the peach than the delicacy of the wild rose; and her figure was far too slender to excite admiration. She had once heard herself described, disparagingly, as "a brown slip of a girl," and accepted the criticism humbly as a painful truth.

The tossing and turning of her restless night had tousled her hair to such a degree that it took a long time to comb smooth again, and she was still dealing with the last tangles when Major Bradwell came in, stooping beneath the low lintel of the doorway. He straightened up and then for a long moment stood looking at her where she sat by the table, comb in one hand and mirror in the other, and her hair tumbled about her shoulders. There was a curious expression in his eyes, as though he were really seeing her for the first time, and he seemed to be about to speak, but then the tavern-keeper came forward to ask how soon he desired the horses to be saddled, and he answered that question instead.

"As soon as Miss Hallett has broken her fast. Have your wife serve her at once." He turned to Imelda, brisk and formal as before. "The rain has stopped, but the road is a quagmire and we shall make but a poor pace. Best to set out as soon as we can."

She nodded, putting down comb and mirror to gather up her hair and coil and twist it into its knot high at the back of her head. He was still watching her, and she was disconcerted to find that her fingers were trembling as she pinned the knot into place; yet she had spoken truly when she told Jedediah that she was not afraid of Major Bradwell. She did not know what it was that was making her heart race and her fingers shake, but it was certainly not fear.

"There is a lad here who attends to the heavy work," the Major went on, "and I have hired him to take the place of your servant as far as your kinsman's house. Then he will bring the horse back so that your man may follow you as soon as he is able to ride. The boy will be able to tell him the way."

"Thank you," Imelda replied inadequately. It was the only answer she could think of, for she was still wondering what he had been about to say when the tavern-keeper interrupted, and she felt certain that the question would continue to tease her for a long time to come.

The old woman set a scanty and unappetizing meal before her, and Imelda ate sparingly of it. Another thought occurred to her, and she looked with faint misgivings at Giles.

"What has become of those two men?"

"Gone," he replied briefly. "I would have preferred to hand them over to the law, but there is neither Justice nor Constable within miles of this place, and I cannot afford the time it would take to deal with the matter. I must be in Plymouth before nightfall."

"Is your home there, sir?" she ventured.

He shook his head. "No, madam, I am attached to the garrison. That is why I am not at liberty to delay long enough to see those two louts delivered to justice. I make you my apologies. They merit severe punishment."

He seemed to have the trick of making remarks to which one could find no answer. Imelda did not care whether or not her two tormentors were punished, as long as Jedediah recovered and she was not obliged to encounter them again, but it was plain that Major Bradwell thought otherwise.

Aware of his impatience to be gone, she finished her meal quickly and got up. Bradwell nodded to the tavern-keeper and himself took her saddle-bags out to the stable, leaving Imelda to put on her cloak and take leave of Jedediah. She hated to abandon him to the doubtful care of the old woman, but was practical enough to accept that this was the only possible course.

She heard the horses being brought from the ramshackle outbuilding where they had been stabled, and with a final word of encouragement and farewell to Jedediah went across to the door as Major Bradwell appeared again on the threshold. The double-gelding was outside, with a lad of some fourteen years already in the saddle, and the old man was holding the bridle of a powerful chestnut stallion of a quality which indicated that the Major had not only an eye for a good mount, but also a purse deep enough to enable him to indulge it. The chestnut was one of the finest horses Imelda had ever seen.

The ground outside the door was inches deep in mire, and before she could take a step forward Giles swept her up in his arms and strode through the squelching mud to set her on the gelding's back. Imelda gasped, and thanked him in some confusion, for, taken completely by surprise, she had instinctively clasped an arm about his neck. Now she would have been

willing to swear that, regarding him at such discon-
certingly close quarters, she had seen an unexpected
gleam of amusement in his eyes.

It was several minutes before she dared to look
at him again, and then she stole a cautious glance at
him as he rode beside her. She could see only his
profile, and that seemed as stern and aloof as ever,
so perhaps she had imagined that reassuring glint of
humour. She sighed, and wondered if he was going
to ride all the way to Conyngton St. John in forbidding
silence.

She would have been astonished to learn that behind the austere façade he was almost as much at a
loss as she was herself. The truth was that Giles Bradwell was unaccustomed to the company of young
gentlewomen. He came of a wealthy family of the
merchant class, and had been only sixteen when he
entered the army; Cromwell's army; the "New Model"
which had brought down a monarchy and executed
a King, and was still the most powerful weapon in
the hands of the man, now Lord Protector of England, who had created it.

Now Giles was twenty-five, and nine years of hard
soldiering, at home in England and in Ireland, had
left him little time to practise social graces. There
had been women in his life, of course, as there were
in the life of any young man of normal appetites, even
in "the army of the Saints," but none of them had
been girls like Imelda Hallett. A lady, a Royalist, and,
for the time being, completely dependent upon his
protection, she was something entirely new in his experience. He could deal with brisk efficiency with the

difficulties confronting her, but he did not know how to talk to her.

Yet from that unpromising beginning there grew between them, as the slow miles fell behind, a degree of understanding which neither of them, the previous night, would have believed to be possible; imperceptibly, and yet so swiftly that the thing had happened before they were aware of it, a bond was established which took no account of differences of birth or loyalty or tradition. The first link had been forged by that long exchange of glances when he came back into the tavern as she sat combing her hair; the second when he lifted her on to the horse; the third, perhaps, at the moment when, emerging from the maze of deep Devon lanes in which Imelda and Jedediah had wandered blindly the day before, they found before them a more open prospect and country of a very different character.

It rose to a distant, forbidding horizon; a high, bleak skyline of moor and crag, with rainclouds still dragging their tattered grey skirts across it; a wild and somehow savage-looking region that stretched beyond the range of vision and seemed to lie like a gigantic barrier directly across their path. Imelda gasped, and turned a dismayed look towards her companion.

"What place is that?"

"Dartmoor," he replied briefly, and the boy who rode before Imelda said with shrill alarm:

"I be'ant going nigh the Moor! There be ghosties

and goblins there, and 'tis said that o' winter nights 'ee can hear the Hounds."

"The Hounds?" Imelda repeated apprehensively.

"Aye, the Yeth Hounds! The Devil's pack, hunting among the tors."

"Enough!" Giles put in sternly, and smiled with reassurance and understanding into Imelda's frightened eyes. "The Moor *is* dangerous, but because of perils of an earthly kind. Bogs that can swallow both horse and rider; mists that come down without warning, so that a traveller becomes utterly lost and wanders ever deeper into a waste of rock and heather; but the road we follow merely skirts the edge of the Moor. You have nothing to fear."

Nothing to fear. Imelda, meeting the steady gaze of the blue-grey eyes, faced at last the inner certainty which, deny it as she might, had been with her from the moment of their meeting. The sense of sure protection, and of burdens lifted from her by a stranger who somehow was no stranger at all.

After that it was easy enough to talk. The intangible barriers of divergent loyalties which at first had loomed so formidably between them no longer seemed of any importance, and they were simply a young man and a young woman exploring a ripening acquaintance and finding mutual delight in it. She learned that his home was in Bristol, where his family had been shipbuilders for more than a hundred years, and that though he was an only son, his father had yielded to his burning desire to follow a military career. In return she told him a little about her own family, of the change in her own life which Sir Darrell Conyngton's offer had

brought about, and even admitted briefly some of the
doubts and fears which the unknown future inspired
in her. Yet, even as she spoke, she realized that these
had been overwhelmed by the chilling knowledge that,
once established in her kinsman's fiercely Royalist
household, she could have no hope of ever meeting
Major Giles Bradwell again.

Sir Darrell's house was situated on that side of
Conyngton St. John by which Imelda and Giles approached, so that they came to it without actually
passing through the village. A labourer working in
one of the fields bordering the road told them how
to reach it, and following his directions they rode
down a hill into a wooded hollow where a brook
tumbled across the road. Splashing through the hurrying water, they began to climb again across the shoulder of another hill, and as they emerged from the
trees they could see, above them on their right, the
burned-out shell of a great house crowning its crest.
Imelda caught her breath.

"Conyngton!" she said in a whisper. "That was once
my kinsman's home."

Giles cast the place a frowning glance. "What came
to it? The wars?"

She nodded. "It was sacked and burned in '43.
There is only the Dower House left." She hesitated.
"Major Bradwell, it may be that you will be made
greatly unwelcome there. I am sorry."

He had still been frowning at the death's-head ruin
above them, but now turned quickly to Imelda again.
The wistful note in her voice had not escaped him,

and it was a measure of the understanding already reached between them that he knew she was thinking not merely of now, but of the future. He was thinking the same thing himself, with a degree of dismay that startled him.

"Small wonder if I am not, after *that*," he replied, with a jerk of his head towards the ruined house. "I would find it hard myself to forgive such a loss." He saw that trouble still lingered in her face, and added reassuringly: "Have no fear. Whatever manner of greeting Sir Darrell may accord me will be spoken to Giles Bradwell, and not to an officer of the Plymouth garrison."

"Thank you." Imelda's voice was not quite steady. "You are generous, sir."

He shook his head in quick dissent, and was silent while they rounded the shoulder of the hill and saw before them the gateway the countryman had described. Beyond it, a track wound through a narrow, sheltering belt of woodland, and then the Dower House was before them, on the other side of a strip of parkland. A handsome, timbered building with mullioned windows, and graceful chimneys soaring above a many-gabled roof; a pleasant garden surrounded it, with a glimpse of orchard beyond, and in front was a stone-flagged forecourt from which a few shallow steps led up to the front door.

They dismounted, leaving the boy in charge of the horses, and in silence went up the steps. Imelda's heart was pounding again, and some of her apprehension returned as Giles rapped on the door. How would she be received, arriving thus, escorted only by a Roundhead officer?

The door was opened by a manservant whose eyes widened with shock at sight of the scarlet coat, and then narrowed as his face settled into an expression of wary politeness. Giles nodded to him, and firmly ushered Imelda into the house, saying pleasantly as he did so:

"Good-day to you, friend. Be good enough to inform Sir Darrell Conyngton that his kinswoman, Miss Hallett, has arrived."

The man flashed a startled glance from the speaker to Imelda, but before he could reply a door on the far side of the square hall was flung open and a man clad in rusty black emerged, turning on the threshold angrily to address someone still within the room.

"And I warn you again, Sir Darrell, that I am right and you wrong! This parish is accursed by witchcraft, by an abomination of evil which must be rooted out and destroyed, ere it destroy us all and sink us into everlasting Hell. As the squire, you have a duty to perform! A duty to God, and to those of your people as yet untainted by the deadly poison spreading throughout this place. A duty! Neglect it at your peril."

Without waiting for an answer, or perhaps expecting none, he swung round again into the hall and so became aware of Giles and Imelda, staring at him in the blankest astonishment. For an instant he checked, and stared in his turn, a lean, angular man of middle height, with a thin-lipped, down curving mouth, a lantern jaw blue from the razor, and burning, fanatical eyes. For a second or two his smouldering glance rested

upon Giles, flickered briefly to the girl, and then returned to the soldier.

"Who you may be, sir, I know not," he declaimed,
"but take heed of what I say! This is a place accursed,
where Satan goeth raging up and down, seeking whom
he may devour. There be those here who serve and
worship him with horrid blasphemy, to the great sorrow and suffering of the Lord's elect, but behold! I
hear him not. I will go forth against him, alone if
need be, armed with the sword of vengeance and the
breastplate of righteousness, until he and all his
minions are driven back into the Pit from whence they
came."

Again he did not wait for a reply, but strode past
them to the door which the servant was still holding
open, but before this could be closed behind him he
swung round again, raising a pointing finger at Imelda
in so menacing a fashion that she instinctively shrank
closer to Giles. It seemed, however, that the other's
purpose was warning rather than accusation.

"If this woman be in your charge, sir, I counsel you
to take her hence without delay, for it is ever the
weaker vessel that falls victim to the blandishments of
the foul Fiend. Take her hence, I say, lest by damnable
witchcraft she imperil her immortal soul."

He stalked off down the steps and out of sight. As
the servant closed the door, Giles said curtly:

"Who is that man?"

"That be our preacher, sir. Dr. Malperne," the man
replied woodenly. "I'll tell Sir Darrell you be here,
sir."

"There is no need." The voice, courteous but very

cold, spoke from the direction of the room from which Malperne had emerged, and Imelda, looking quickly round, saw that a man who must be Sir Darrell himself was standing in the doorway.

The squire of Conyngton St. John was nearly as tall as Giles, and only seven or eight years older. Hair of reddish gold fell in ordered curls over his lace collar, framing a strong, stern face, and though his clothes were well worn there was an air of elegance about him. He came slowly towards them, paying no heed to Imelda but watching the red-coated officer with the same sort of wariness his servant had shown.

"Sir Darrell Conyngton?" Giles inquired courteously, adding, as the other man inclined his head: "I bring you your kinswoman, sir, Miss Hallett, whom I understand to be expected here."

"Imelda Hallett?" Astonishment deepened in Conyngton's hazel eyes as he glanced at the girl; astonishment and a hint of suspicion. "Why then, you are welcome, cousin, but how is this? Do you travel unattended by any servant?"

She curtsied silently, not knowing how to reply, but Giles was still easily in command, identifying himself to Sir Darrell, explaining how he had found Miss Hallett lost and benighted at a wayside ale-house, her servant injured and helpless after "an accident."

"She told me, sir, whither she was bound, and since I am on my way to Plymouth I thought it best to bring her to you. That ale-house was no place for a gentlewoman."

"I am most grateful to you, Major Bradwell." The suspicion had faded from Sir Darrell's eyes and he spoke less coldly, though still with a marked degree of reserve in his manner. "Pray come within." He glanced at the waiting servant. "Inform her ladyship, and then bring wine to the parlour."

He took Imelda's hand and led her to the room from which he had emerged. Giles followed, and they were scarcely within the parlour before Lady Conyngton joined them, for she had observed their arrival from an upper window. She was a tall, graceful, slightly foreign-looking young woman with a striking, aquiline face, dark eyes and heavy black hair, and Imelda thought with a touch of panic that she could very easily be intimidating.

Nothing, however, could have been kinder than her welcome. She exclaimed over the girl's misadventure as described by Giles, thanked him for his care of her, and bore her away with her to put off her cloak. Giles, more than a little dismayed at seeing Imelda whisked so promptly from his presence, without even a chance to say farewell, accepted a glass of wine from Sir Darrell and did his best to describe the exact location of the ale-house where Jedediah had been left.

"I know the place," Conyngton said finally, after a question or two, "and you are quite right, Major. It is not fit lodging for a gentlewoman." He frowned. "Nor for a sick man, either. Aid must be sent to him. What is the nature of his injury?"

Giles hesitated for a moment, for he had no wish to go into details of the scene he had interrupted, or to boast of himself as Imelda's saviour. "A blow on the head," he said at length. "Last night he knew us not, but this morning his senses had returned, though

he will be in no case to travel for some few days."
Then, because he was anxious to leave the subject,
and because the encounter with Dr. Malperne had left
a faint, lingering uneasiness in his mind, he came
abruptly to a different matter. "Your preacher, sir,
seems greatly exercised over the question of witches—
and rightly so, if there be any in this parish."

"Say rather 'in Malperne's own mind,'" Sir Darrell
replied impatiently. "I believe him honest in his con-
victions, but sadly mistaken. We have never been
troubled by such evil here."

"Never?" Giles's brows lifted. "You are confident,
sir."

"Never within living memory," Conyngton assured
him. "Oh, there is an old crone who is the village
wise woman, and deals in herbs and simples. No doubt
some of the young maids go to her to learn whom they
will marry, as their mothers went before them—and
no doubt their grandmothers, too, for she is very old.
But witchcraft? No."

Giles was silent for a moment, frowning at the wine
in his glass. A staunch but moderate Parliamentarian,
he was first and foremost a soldier, a professional fight-
ing-man with scant sympathy for the various fanatical
religious sects of which much of the New Model Army
was composed, but his nine years' service had given
him a wide and varied experience of them. That Puritan
preacher was just such a fanatic; one who would pursue
what he believed to be his appointed path reckless of
what might come of it. Such men were dangerous and
Giles was wondering how to offer a warning to this
proud Royalist in a way which would not give offence.

"Such godly zeal as your preacher's is admirable, Sir Darrell," he said carefully after a pause, "but may sometimes be misguided. I have seen the witch-hunters at work, and I know that when fear of witchcraft is in, good sense is often out, so that the innocent suffer along with the guilty. Your wise woman would do well to cease her trafficking before it brings grave harm to her, and to others."

Whether the warning was accepted or resented he never knew, for at that moment Lady Conyngton came back into the room. Crossing it to where the two men stood near the fireplace, she held out her hand to Giles, her dark eyes lifted to his in a steady look.

"Miss Hallett has told me, Major Bradwell," she said quietly. "I had not realized how great a debt of gratitude she owes to you."

Giles, embarrassed, and wishing that Imelda had withheld her confidence until after his departure, took the proffered hand briefly in his and bowed over it, while Lady Conyngton, in a few vivid sentences, described the situation to her husband. Sir Darrell looked at him with more friendliness in his eyes than Giles had yet seen there, and with a measure of respect, too, for his reticence.

"I will not embarass you with thanks, Major," he said, "but know that my cousin's debt is ours also, and will not be forgotten."

Giles shook his head. "I am glad, sir, that I was able to be of service to Miss Hallett, and I have only one regret. That I was unable to deliver up to justice the louts who attacked her."

Lady Conyngton's gaze, kindly and very faintly

amused, rested thoughtfully upon him. "I imagine, Major, that they did not escape altogether unscathed. I am told that you administered summary punishment in a masterly fashion."

"Far less than they deserved, madam," he replied grimly. He paused, and then with an air of decision set down his empty glass. "Permit me to take leave of your ladyship. I have duties awaiting me in Plymouth."

"Stay a few minutes longer, sir," she replied. "Miss Hallett, I am sure, will wish to take leave of you. At present my woman is attending upon her, but she will join us again directly."

He was more than willing to linger, though he was able to dissemble this and give merely a courteous reply. Sir Darrell spoke again of Jedediah and this subject occupied them until Imelda came back into the room, her hair freshly dressed and the splashes of mud removed from her shoes and shabby gown. Her glance flew at once to Giles, as though in relief at finding him still there.

"In good time, cousin," Sir Darrell greeted her kindly. "Major Bradwell is waiting to take leave of you."

"I am glad that you stayed for me, sir." Imelda heard her own voice speaking as though it belonged to someone else, heard it saying the correct, formal things, in spite of the tight knot of misery inside her. "I have not yet thanked you for turning aside from your own journey to bring me here."

"It was a pleasure to do so, madam," he replied, equally formal. "And now that your travels are safely over, I trust that you will soon be able to forget the disagreeable events which attended them."

"I may forget that, sir, but not your kindness, and your care of me." She put out her hand to him, looking up into his face; her voice shook a little. "I shall never forget."

His hand closed over hers, and held it for a moment; she thought she heard him say, under his breath, "Nor I," but she could not be sure, and next moment he was bowing to Lady Conyngton, speaking more formal words of farewell, and then going with Sir Darrell out of the room. Imelda stood staring blindly before her, hearing only the firm footsteps and faint jingle of spurs going away from her across the hall. She could think of nothing else, was aware of nothing else, not even of the sympathy and humourous understanding in Charity Conyngton's dark eyes.

Part 2

It appeared to Imelda, accustomed to her own poverty-stricken home, that the household at the Dower House was considerable, for on the morning after her arrival, when Lady Conyngton conducted her over the house, there seemed to be servants everywhere, and the thought that she was to assume a position of authority over them, second only to that of their mistress, was a daunting one.

She was taken first of all to the nursery, for Charity, like all mothers, was eager to show off her children. There were three of them. Young Darrell, the heir, was a sturdy handsome little boy of three, with his mother's black hair, and fine hazel eyes like Sir Darrell's, while two-year-old Margaret had the red-gold curls which, as Imelda was to discover, were a family characteristic. The baby, Anne, was still in the cradle. Imelda was enchanted with all three, for she loved children, and the parting from her brother's little ones, who had been much in her care, had been the bitterest wrench of all when she left her home.

Their tour of the house brought them eventually to the stillroom, where the household medicines and cordials and other remedies were made, as well as perfumes and toilet waters for my lady's use. Charity led the way in, but then halted and said sharply to someone already in the room:

"Rebecca! I did not expect to find you here."

Imelda thought she sounded not displeased, but just a little put out, with the faintest hint of dismay behind the words, and, looking past her, saw that one of the maids was standing near the window, measuring some liquid from a flask into a small glass vial. She was holding the vessel at eye level, and Imelda could see her in profile against the light, a tall, thin woman of middle age, with boldly carved features which gave her a somewhat predatory look and yet were gauntly handsome.

"I'm putting up the medicines your ladyship commanded," she replied. "For the sick children at the mill."

She spoke politely, but without looking round, and it struck Imelda as odd that a servant should be so lacking in courtesy to her mistress, even taking into account the task in which she was engaged. Nor was her voice like those of the other maidservants they had encountered that morning; it was the voice of an educated woman. She heard Lady Conyngton say:

"Of course. I had forgotten. Be sure that you instruct their mother carefully." Her voice sounded quite composed now, but she laid her hand on Imelda's arm, gripping it firmly as though in restraint or warning as she went on: "Miss Hallett, this is Rebecca Moone, my excellent stillroom maid. You will find that she is greatly skilled in everything pertaining to the art."

The glass vial was full now. Rebecca Moone lowered it, turning with slow deliberation to face them, and Imelda with difficulty suppressed an exclamation as Charity's fingers pressed still harder on her arm, for that side of the woman's face which had been turned from them was hideously disfigured. A great scar—or a burn, it would appear—spread right across it and down her neck, twisting her mouth awry and puckering the discoloured flesh into grotesque bumps and ridges that disappeared finally beneath her close lined cap and broad, high collar.

Miraculously, her sight had been spared, but as Imelda met the eyes that looked out of that wreck of a face she was conscious of a chill of revulsion even stronger than that occasioned by the disfigurement itself. Never in her life had she seen such eyes. Of a strange, light grey that was bright yet somehow opaque, like the shine on a new silver coin, they seemed to hide the thoughts behind them and yet to bore straight into her own, detecting her shock and horror and pity, and rejecting all three with contempt and bitter mockery. For one brief fraction of time it seemed to Imelda that she could see nothing but those eyes; that her will was subjugated and held captive by the power of them. Then the woman looked away, putting down the flask to stopper the neck of the vial, and the spell was broken. Imelda swallowed, and managed to say in a more less normal tone:

"I shall be happy to learn of her. My own knowledge is not as great as I could wish."

There was a little more talk between her ladyship and the maid, and then they were out of the stillroom and going through the house towards the parlour. Not until they reached it did Charity speak again, and then she said apologetically:

"I am sorry for that. I intended to warn you about Rebecca before you saw her."

Imelda was still subdued and shaken by the encounter, and found it difficult to reply in a matter-of-fact way. She could not shake off the effect of the woman's eyes.

"It is a terrible affliction," she said in a low voice. "How did it happen?"

Charity shook her head, sitting down and motioning to Imelda to do the same. "I do not know. She never speaks of it, and I do not question her. From the appearance of the scar she must have suffered the injury some years ago, long before we found her."

"Before you *found* her?"

"Yes, under a bush by the roadside, one bitter day two winters since. She was destitute and starving, and close to death when we brought her in, but when she recovered a little she told me that she is a widow whose husband left nothing but debts, so that she found herself homeless and penniless when he died. Because of her looks, no one would take her in, even as a servant, and she had been wandering for months, begging her bread from door to door until her strength gave out. We nursed her back to health, and for very pity I could not drive her forth again."

Imelda was silent, reflecting with humility that she would not have had so much compassion, or perhaps such strength of mind. She ought to pity Rebecca Moone, and yet even the thought of the woman aroused only horror, and dismay that they must live under the same roof. Despising herself, she said in a small voice:

"Yet she does not seem like a servant."

"No, it is plain that she had known better days, but she never speaks of the past and I respect her reticence. It cannot have been happy. She seems content enough here, though she is a solitary creature and happiest roaming the woods and meadows, by day or night, gathering plants and herbs for her distilling. The other servants do not like her, and some of them, I believe, even fear her a little."

Imelda felt that she could sympathize with them, and then was instantly ashamed of the thought. She found that Lady Conyngton was regarding her with a good deal of comprehension and just a hint of reproof, and both these qualities were evident in her voice as she continued quietly:

"Rebecca's disfigurement must always be a shock to those who see it for the first time, but you must endeavour to grow accustomed to it. She has a heavy enough cross to bear without being constantly reminded of the repulsion her looks inspire."

Imelda flushed scarlet. "I will try, my lady," she murmured, and then, in an attempt at self-justification, added with a rush: "Truth to tell, it was not so much her disfigurement that shocked me, as her eyes. You will think me foolish, but they—they seem scarcely human."

Charity smiled faintly. "I think you fanciful, my dear. Rebecca is human enough, poor soul, and has known her share of human suffering. We who are more fortunate must endeavour not to add to it."

To Imelda's relief, for she felt that this conversation was doing her no good in Lady Conyngton's eyes, they were interrupted at this point by a knocking at the front door. A woman's voice was heard speaking to the servant who answered the summons, and then there were light, hurrying footsteps in the hall and a girl in a blue riding-habit came quickly into the room.

She was about Imelda's age, small and slender and grey-eyed, with a high-crown, plumed hat set upon auburn curls, and she entered with outstretched hands, and with impetuous words already upon her lips.

"Charity, is all well with you? I have just heard that there is talk in the village of red-coat soldiers coming here yesterday."

Lady Conyngton laughed, rising to take the new-comer's hands in her own. "By my faith, how swiftly rumours grow! Only one soldier, Roxanne, and he upon a most kindly errand. He brought our kins-woman, Miss Hallett, safely to us."

The younger woman stared for a moment, and then she, too, began to laugh. "The village will have it that there was a whole troop, at least, summoned by Dr. Malperne to search out witches. Though why they should seek them at the Dower House, and nowhere else, no one has yet thought fit to explain. I gave no credence to *that*, but I knew something must have set such a rumour afoot, and feared the soldiers might have come here on some other errand."

The latter words were spoken more gravely, and Charity was as grave as she nodded her understanding. There had been an abortive Royalist rising in the West Country barely a month before; in Devon it had been defeated by Commonwealth troops and now its leaders were prisoners in Exeter. Imelda, remembering this, and seeing the sober glance her companions exchanged, wondered whether Sir Darrell had played a (mercifully undiscovered) part.

Charity turned to beckon her forward. "Imelda, my dear, let me make you known to Mrs. Pennan, my dear neighbour and very dear friend."

Imelda curtsied; Roxanne Pennan gave her a friendly smile, studying her with interest and some curiosity, for which, no doubt, Lady Conyngton's mention of the redcoat soldier was partly responsible. Charity herself seemed to realize this, and related circumstances which had led to Imelda arriving at the Dower House in such unlooked-for company.

"Malperne was here, ranting against witches, at the same time," Charity concluded, "so no doubt that is the source of the rumour you heard."

"He talks of nothing else," Roxanne agreed with a frown, "and now others are beginning to talk of it, too. My maid had a tale yesterday of a cow dying strangely at Whitethorn Farm the day after the farmer drove old Tabitha Spragge away when she went begging there. Now it is being said that she bewitched the beast."

Charity sighed. "Tabitha has been an evil-tempered old beldame ever since I can remember, and the villagers' respect for her has always been tinged with fear, but this talk of casting evil spells is something new."

"I do not wonder that people fear her, for she grows exceeding strange," Roxanne said reflectively. "Last time I saw her she was hobbling along, muttering and laughing aloud although she was quite alone. I wonder that you can bring yourself to visit that cottage of hers. I would not go there."

Charity shrugged. "Someone has to see that she has food and firing. I have known her all my life, and, besides, I have a duty to care for all our people, but I begin to fear for Tabitha. She is the first person Malperne is likely to accuse of witchcraft, should it ever come to naming names."

"You say that he was here yesterday when Miss Hallett arrived?" Roxanne said uneasily. "If this Major Bradwell heard him prating of witches here, might that not bring trouble upon us? Cromwell's soldiers are fierce against anything that savours of witchcraft, whether there is truth in it or not."

"No!" Imelda spoke vehemently, and then blushed furiously as they both looked at her. "I mean, he was not like that. When the boy from the tavern spoke of witches and goblins and the Devil's hounds on Dartmoor, Major Bradwell rebuked him, and said that such tales were told of any wild, uninhabited place."

"I do not think he set much store by what he heard,"

Charity agreed, "for Darrell told me afterwards that he spoke of Malperne, saying that though such godly zeal is admirable, it can sometime be misguided, so it seems that the Major is no fanatic. I believe we have no cause to fear him."

The next day was Sunday, and the weather had remained dull and wet. Roxanne arrived in a handsome coach to carry Lady Conyngton and Imelda with her to church in the village, Sir Darrell accompanying them on horseback. He no longer kept a coach of his own, and although the Pennans' house lay nearer than the Dower House to the village, it was apparently Roxanne's custom to take Charity up with her when the weather was bad.

There was another coach already outside the church when they arrived, and Imelda wondered fleetingly to whom it belonged. There were one or two riding horses as well, but most of the parishioners appeared to come on foot. Following her companions into the church, she saw that it had been stripped bare in the Puritan fashion, with the walls whitewashed, and plain windows instead of the jewel colours of stained glass. There were two large pews, one obviously belonging to the squire and his family; the other, slightly smaller, might be presumed the property of the owner of the second coach, but as the wooden walls of both rose higher than a man's head, it was impossible to see who this might be; the rest of the congregation stood, or sat on benches around the walls.

To Puritans, preaching was far more important than praying, and Imelda was not in the least surprised that Dr. Malperne's sermon should comprise the principal part of the service. In her own village the Anglican parson had long since been driven out, and his place taken by a preacher who had once been one of Cromwell's troopers, and she might even have accounted Conyngton St. John more fortunate than her own old home in that Dr. Malperne was obviously a man of education, had the content of his sermon been other than it was. She was prepared for Old Testament savagery, for warnings of God's vengeance and threats of Hell-fire; she would not even have been surprised to hear a political harangue; what she had not expected, however, was a thundering denunciation of witchcraft, and accusations which, while naming no names, seemed to embrace the whole parish.

Conyngton St. John, according to its minister, was given over to lewdness and depravity, looking back with sinful yearning to the evil days of King and bishop, and to pagan festivals of Yule-tide and harvest-home, of church-ales and maypole dancing. It was no wonder that in soil so fertile in wickedness the infinitely greater evil of witchcraft should have takén root, and was now spreading its poisonous tendrils throughout the whole community.

"For make no mistake, there are many among us who traffic with the foul Fiend, and by their evil sorceries cause the powers of Hell to walk alive upon the earth. Who are they? you may ask. How may we know them? Alas Satan their master teaches them something of his own deceit, for is he not the Prince of Lies? It may be that your neighbour is one such, or your trusted friend—nay, even those closest to you by ties of blood cannot be above suspicion. And if suspicion come, then it must be voiced, so that a full and proper trial may be made and the truth of guilt or innocence be established. This evil must be rooted out, these servants of the Devil exposed and destroyed, no matter who they may be."

Imelda saw Sir Darrell shift angrily in his seat, and he and Charity exchange a troubled glance. She could not wonder at their disquiet. Whether or not it were Malperne's purpose to do so, the sermon he was preaching now could not be more surely designed to stir up trouble in a small community already uneasy and frightened. She remembered how he had told the squire it was his duty to move against the witches, a duty he would neglect at his peril. Was this his way of making good that threat?

By the time the sermon was over—and it lasted a full two hours—she could feel tension in the church as though it were something tangible; tangible and frightening; and when she and Roxanne, who had shared the Conyngton pew with them, followed Darrell and Charity from the church, she could see that many of the congregation (none of whom would have dreamed of leaving before the squire and his lady) were looking side-long at one another as though Malperne's words had already taken possession of their minds. The minister himself had moved to the door to accord his parishioners the courtesy of a word with them as they left, and Darrell paused when he reached him. From his commanding height he looked down at Malperne, his expression even more stern than usual.

"I cannot commend you upon your sermon, sir," he informed him coldly, "for I had seldom heard anything more surely calculated to sow discord and suspicion. What purpose do you think to serve by it?"

The minister drew himself up and met the stern gaze with one of his burning stares. "My purpose, Sir Darrell? It is to bring the evil out of the darkness into the light of day. To teach these misguided people that nothing, neither considerations of loyalty nor of family duty, matter beside the need to purge ourselves of this abomination which has come among us. If any think they have knowledge of those who are the Devil's agents upon earth, they must speak, so that the truth may be laid bare before all."

"If any think they have knowledge!" Darrell repeated impatiently. "If they *think* it! Do you not see that in urging this you are opening the door to malice and envy and the paying-off of old scores? If there indeed be witches here, which I take leave to doubt—"

"*If* there be witches?" The interruption, bitterly spoken in a woman's voice, came from immediately behind them and brought Imelda swinging round. "Of a certainty there are, Darrell Conyngton, and you know it as well as I."

The speaker, who must have emerged from the second pew and followed them to the door, was a short, very stout, middle-aged woman all in sombre black, the heavy weeds and veil of a widow. She must have been handsome once, before time and increasing girth robbed her of her looks, but there was something repellent in the hard, humourless line of her lips and the look of implacable hatred in her eyes. Behind her, a slight, fair-haired young woman, also in widow's weeds, held the hands of two small boys.

Sir Darrell bowed slightly, but answered as coldly as he had spoken to Dr. Malperne. "I know nothing of the sort, madam. Neither, I imagine, do you, but if you do possess such knowledge, then no doubt you will disclose it to the proper authorities so that they may judge of its worth."

"Be sure I should! That I shall, as soon as I can discover but one of these vile hags. One thing I know, and that is that the evil we speak of is no recent thing. I have not forgotten how my son died, even if you pretend to."

Imelda saw Sir Darrell stiffen, but before he could speak, Charity's hand, resting lightly on his arm, tightened its grip, and she said in a level voice:

"Jonas's death was an accident, aunt. Those who found him—*your* friends and servants, I would remind you—affirmed that. Why will you not accept that it is so?"

"An accident!" The other woman almost spat the words at her. "He was murdered, and by witchcraft as like as not. What else but foul sorceries could have lured him to that place at such a time, or called up the storm that brought about his death?"

"Mrs. Shenfield," Malperne put in earnestly, "these are grave charges, but against whom? Who in this parish do you accuse?"

"Who?" A look of cunning flickered across the woman's face. "Nay, sir, when I can tell you that, be sure that I shall speak. Until then I keep my own counsel."

She nodded at him, as though to emphasize her words, and then thrust between him and the Conyngtons and marched along the path towards the lychgate. The young widow with the little boys hesitated, casting a pleading look at Charity; it seemed as though she were about to speak, but the older woman, looking round, called sharply, "Come, Ellen," and with a little helpless shrug the fair girl hurried after her.

The preacher watched them go and then turned again to Darrell. "You see, sir, others beside myself— and not only ignorant, humble folk—perceive the evil to which you deliberately blind your eyes."

"Dr. Malperne!" Again it was Charity who replied. "My aunt Elizabeth has never reconciled herself to the loss of her son. He was ever her favourite, especially after her daughters became estranged from her, and his sudden death, in circumstances which have never been explained, had a grievous effect upon her. At first she tried to blame us. Failing in that, she has for years been seeking another scapegoat, which she finds now in these rumours of witchcraft."

"And who is to say, my lady, that she is mistaken?" he retorted. "You admit that there is a mystery surrounding Jonas Shenfield's death, and it may well be that those circumstances which have always perplexed us are due to the horrible practices of witches. Oh, this unhappy place, if the evil is indeed so deep-rooted! May the Lord strengthen me, his servant, that I may be victorious over the powers of darkness!"

Sir Darrell inclined his head abruptly to the minister and moved away along the path with Charity at his side and Imelda and Roxanne following, while the rest of the congregation, who had been pressing as close behind them as respect permitted, began to stream after them. Outside the lych-gate, Mrs. Shenfield stood waiting beside her coach, in which her young companion and the children were already seated, but she ignored the party from the Dower House as completely as though they did not exist. Imelda wondered why she had delayed, but a moment later the reason became apparent as two serving-men hurried up and began to assist her to climb into the vehicle, which, because of her girth, she could not do unaided. It seemed a ridiculous anticlimax to the scene in the church porch, but any amusement Imelda might have felt was banished as, with the lady in the coach at last and the door shut, one of the servants turned in their direction.

He was a lanky fellow, possibly between thirty and forty years of age, with cropped, sandy-coloured hair and a gaunt, unprepossessing face, but it was his eyes, and the expression in them, which caught her attention. Pale blue in colour, they blazed with a malevolence which seemed to hover on the brink of madness, but after the first shocked instant she realized that the man was not looking at her, but past her to where Sir Darrell was handing his wife up into the coach. Imelda had the curious impression that the man saw nothing else, was aware of nothing but them, and she continued to watch him until Darrell, having handed Roxanne, too, into the coach, turned to her. He was obliged to touch her lightly on the arm to attract her attention, and when he did she started and shivered.

"Cousin," she whispered, "who is that man, that

servant who stares so in this direction?"

He glanced towards the other coach, and a quick frown came. "His name is Daniel Stotewood," he replied curtly. "As arrant a knave as ever walked the earth, and as insolent as he is cunning. He is in service at the Moat House."

He helped her into the coach and then moved away to mount his horse. Imelda, looking back as the cumbersome vehicle lurched forward, saw that Daniel Stotewood had turned away and attached himself to the fringe of a group of men and women in the same dark, plain livery as his own, but the memory of him lingered unpleasantly in her mind, and she could not shake off a feeling of disquiet. The Dower House was a pleasant place where she believed she could be happy, but in the village dark forces seemed to be stirring, so that the minister's warning of witches at work suddenly seemed only too likely to be true.

When they had been set down at the Dower House, and taken leave of Mrs. Pennan, Charity took Imelda into the parlour and made her sit down beside her on a daybed near the fire.

"Since this is to be your home, Imelda," she said without preamble, "it is right that you should be informed of certain things. My aunt, Elizabeth Shenfield, whom you saw at church today, is the widow of my father's dear brother. I was orphaned at birth, and penniless, and was brought up in my uncle's household with his own children. That was at the Moat House, a mile or so from here—you must have ridden past its gates on the day Major Bradwell brought you to us. I had three cousins. Beth, now the wife of Sir Richard Linslade of Dorringford, near Exeter. Sarah, who"—she hesitated for a second and then went on—"who is at present living in Holland, and Jonas, the eldest, my uncle's only son. It was his widow, and his two little boys, who were with my aunt at church."

She paused and sat gazing into the fire, and Imelda, watching her, knew that for the moment she had been forgotten. She waited patiently, eager to hear more yet unwilling to intrude, until at last the elder woman sighed, and turned to her again with a faint, rueful smile at her own abstraction.

"It is not necessary to describe to you all the events which led finally to my marriage with Sir Darrell, but you must understand that even in childhood—there was but a year between them in age—my cousin Jonas hated and resented him. Jonas spent much time in Plymouth, with his mother's two brothers who were prosperous merchants there, for he was their heir. They had embraced the Puritan faith, and under their influence Jonas presently did likewise. That was shortly before the late wars.

"There is no need for me to tell *you*, Imelda, how those wars changed the fortunes of Royalist and Roundhead. It is enough to say that by the time Darrell came home again, Jonas exceeded him in wealth and influence, though he could never rob him of the love and loyalty of the people here, for the Conyngtons have been squires of Conyngton St. John for generations. What he *could* do, for he was head of the family by then, was to forbid our marriage, knowing how ardently we both desired it."

"Out of malice?" Imelda asked incredulously, for if Charity, like herself, had been dowerless, surely her guardian ought to have welcomed such a match for her. She knew that her own father would, for any of his daughters.

"Out of malice," Charity agreed. "He stood between us for three bitter years. It may be hard for you to credit so warped a nature, but thus it was. Of latter years, greed and hatred governed his whole life."

"And then he died?"

Charity nodded. "One night he walked out of the Moat House and did not return. Next day his servants, searching for him, found him lying dead in the manor ruins, crushed by a great fall of masonry. There had been a violent gale during the night, and the manor walls had been crumbling dangerously for years, but what took him to such a place at such a time was never discovered." She sighed. "You may imagine the stories which have grown up around the event, for he was bitterly hated here. Now the villagers believe that his ghost roams the ruins, doomed for all eternity to haunt the desolation he created during his life." She read the startled question in Imelda's eyes, and nodded again. "Yes, my dear. It was Jonas who led the Roundhead troop that burned Conyngton."

Imelda stared at her, appalled, not knowing what to say, but beginning to comprehend the magnitude of the gulf which now yawned between Charity Conyngton and the woman who had brought her up. Conyngton St. John was indeed a place divided, the villagers clinging to their old allegiance to the squire, the minister ranging himself on the side of the Puritan household at the Moat House. There was no doubt where her own loyalty must lie, and so the memory of Major Giles Bradwell must be instantly banished from her thoughts whenever it intruded upon them, as it was doing far too often for her peace of mind.

"Jonas's death was a cruel blow to his mother." Charity's quiet voice broke in again upon the confusion of her thoughts. "Had the accident been other than it was, I am certain she would have tried to cast the blame for it upon Darrell and me, but even her own son-in-law, Edward Taynton, who was among those who recovered the body, assured her that no man could either have caused it or prevented it. Now it seems she has seized upon a new possibility to account for what happened that night, and would have it that he was murdered by witchcraft."

"Is it not possible that she may be right?" Imelda suggested tentatively. "You say your cousin was bitterly hated here."

"I cannot believe it!" Charity got up and began to move restlessly about the room. "No one can deny the existence of witches, or of their power to harm, but that there are any here in Conyngton St. John—! Imelda, do you not realize that to believe it is to believe that some of these women, whom I have known all my life, are servants and worshippers of the Devil?"

Imelda was silenced, knowing how reluctant she would be to believe such evil of servants and neighbours at her own old home, and yet the little doubt would not be stifled. Dr. Malperne seemed very sure, and though she instinctively hated and distrusted all

Puritans, she could not help wondering whence that unshakable conviction sprang.

Yet in the days that followed, the dread of witchcraft receded to the very back of her mind as she began to accustom herself to her new life. Her duties were many but none of them were arduous, and far from being regarded as a poor relation accepted on sufferance, she found herself treated very much as though she were a younger sister.

Charity insisted on making her a present of two new gowns, one of a soft lavender blue, the other apricot coloured, and though they were very simple, as befitted her position, the possession of them was overwhelming to a girl who all her life had worn only the cast-off garments of her elder sisters. It ranked with the unheard-of luxury of a bedchamber of her own, for in her father's modest house, more farm than manor, crowded with her parents, her brother and his wife and children, and four unmarried daughters, she had been obliged to share not merely a room, but the bed itself.

The only member of the household with whom she could not feel at ease was Rebecca Moone. She found it difficult to look at the woman's scarred face without an inward shudder, but she thought that in time she could have accustomed herself to the disfigurement. It was still Rebecca's eyes that frightened her. At their second meeting, believing herself the victim of some irrational fancy, she had nerved herself to look straight into them, only to feel again that terrifying sense of subjugation, of enslavement to some uncanny power. No one else seemed to experience a similar reaction, and so thereafter Imelda carefully avoided looking directly at Rebecca, and meanwhile prayed earnestly that she might be delivered from this uncomfortable delusion.

Her feelings towards Rebecca were not her only cause for self-reproach. She had decided that duty, and loyalty to her benefactors, forbade her to think about Giles Bradwell, but it was one thing to make the decision and quite another to abide by it. A dozen times a day the thought of him came into her mind. She could remember, with heart-searing vividness, every detail of the brief time they had spent in each other's company, and found herself picturing a score of different ways in which they might meet again. Neither resolution nor prayer, it seemed, had any effect upon her unruly heart, or the power to control her wayward thoughts.

Meanwhile, life at the Dower House went placidly on. Jedediah, fetched from the ale-house by the manservant sent to help him, had fully recovered from his injury and gone back to Wiltshire, carrying with him letters and loving messages, and a comfortable account of his young mistress's present circumstance to reassure her anxious parents. Dr. Malperne continued to thunder from the pulpit his warnings of witchcraft and his condemnation of all forms of merrymaking, but there had been no more disquieting incidents, and only at the Moat House, it seemed, did he find any sympathy with his views.

Imelda soon learned, with astonishment, that family relationships in Conyngton St. John were even more

complicated than Charity's explanation of the enmity
between Conyngton and Shenfield had led her to suppose. Captain Tom Pennan, Roxanne's sea-faring husband, was Ellen Shenfield's eldest brother, and thus
shared a remote family connection with Charity herself; moreover, the Captain, though a Parliamentarian,
was an old and valued friend of the Conyngtons. Even
more surprising, there appeared to be a bond of sincere
affection between Charity and Ellen.

Imelda, going with her ladyship to Mrs. Pennan's
fine new house nearby (the Captain, at the time of his
marriage, had purchased a few acres from Sir Darrell
in order to build a home for his bride), was startled
to find Ellen there, and to realize that this was no
chance encounter. The young widow had come ex-
pressly to meet Lady Conyngton, and spoke urgently
of the need for Sir Darrell to make some move against
the old wise-woman, Tabitha Spragge.

"Why, Ellen?" Charity demanded sternly. "What
harm has Tabitha ever done to you?"

"None, as yet," Ellen admitted uncomfortably, "but
everybody knows her for a witch—"

"My aunt and Dr. Malperne *think* they know it.
Would you have us hale the poor old creature before
a Justice for no better reason than their prejudice and
her own ill-temper?"

"Do not be angry with me," Ellen said wretchedly.
"You do not realize the danger you court by defending
her, for it is not only Mrs. Shenfield and Dr. Malperne
you have to reckon with. Mr. Taynton is behind them
in this, and you know how much influence *he* wields

in Plymouth. It is in his power to do you serious harm."

"That's true enough," Roxanne agreed. "There is little love lost, either, between Taynton and the Pennan family. He opposes them at every turn, in civic matters as well as in the way of business, so that they are in a fair way to becoming the leaders of opposing factions in the town. That is why the Pennans find it difficult to exert much influence at the Moat House, since Jonas Shenfield left all his affairs in Taynton's hands."

Imelda was puzzled by these references to Taynton. Charity had told her that he was Mrs. Shenfield's son-in-law, yet surely she had said, too, that Jonas Shenfield had had but two sisters? Later, diffidently seeking enlightenment of her ladyship, she received an explanation which, if anything, confused her even more.

"Edward Taynton is my cousin Sarah's husband," Charity told her briefly. "Jonas forced her into the marriage and four years ago she fled to Holland with Hal Mordisford, Sir Darrell's brother-in-law by his first marriage. Hal and Sarah had loved each other for a long time."

Was there no end to it? Imelda thought helplessly. To the tangle of love and hate, of religious and political differences, of friends and enemies inextricably bound by the ties of blood or marriage? It seemed strangely fitting, almost inevitable, that she herself had unwittingly followed the pattern, and now found herself caught fast in a similar snare.

Part 3

One sunny afternoon towards the end of May, when Imelda had been at the Dower House for about six weeks, she was in the garden with the two older children when a servant came to tell her that the Widow Bramble had come from the village and was anxious to speak with Lady Conyngton.

Imelda frowned. "Her ladyship rode out with Sir Darrell more than an hour ago. I do not know when they will return."

"Aye, madam, I know, but Mrs. Bramble seems in sore distress. Should I bid her wait?"

Imelda thought for a moment. Abigail Bramble kept the inn, the Conyngton Arms, and her business must be pressing indeed to bring her toiling on foot up the steep hill to the Dower House on a warm summer day, for she was stout and elderly and seldom went beyond the village. With Lady Conyngton absent, Imelda was her deputy, and her duty was clear.

"I will see Mrs. Bramble," she decided. "Pray take the children back to Nurse, and I will go to her."

It seemed at first, however, that Mrs. Bramble was unwilling to divulge her errand to anyone but Lady Conyngton. She looked doubtfully at Imelda, and shook her head.

"I ought to speak to her ladyship," she said in a troubled voice. "She might not think it fitting for me to talk of such a matter wi' a young lady like you."

"That must be for you to decide, Mrs. Bramble, and of course you may wait for Lady Conyngton to return, if you wish, but are you certain that I can do nothing to help?"

"I be'ant sure anyone can help, madam, but if the wench will heed anyone, she'll heed her ladyship. 'Tis a bad business, but what can't be cured must be endured, and she'll only make matters worse by lying to her father, for he'll have the truth out of her in the end, if he has to thrash her every day for a month." She hesitated, looking worriedly at Imelda, and then added in a burst of confidence: "It be young Matty Weddon, Miss Imelda. She's wi' child."

Imelda stared at her in dismay. She was becoming familiar with the various inhabitants of Conyngton St. John, and she knew immediately whom the widow meant. Matilda Weddon was the blacksmith's only daughter, a pretty, motherless and rather simple girl of sixteen who kept house for her father and two elder brothers; dour, unsociable men, all three, who were respected but not greatly liked by their neighbours. Neither of the young Weddons showed any disposition to marry, and it was generally assumed that Matty, too, would have to remain single, and keep house for the men of her family for the rest of her life. Imelda knew that Charity disapproved of the situation, and had prophesied that no good would come it. Now, it seemed, her misgivings had been justified.

"Does her father know?" she asked Mrs. Bramble, coming straight to what seemed to her the most urgent aspect of the matter.

"The whole village knows," Abigail replied grimly. "She's too far gone to keep it hid any longer, and such a commotion there never was, when Weddon found out how it is with her. Natural enough, he demands to know who get her wi' child, but the wench won't tell. Not that I wonder at that, with those brothers of hers ripe to do murder, but where's the sense in her saying she's lain wi' no man, and that they'd best have a care how they treat her, or they'll be sorry for it? I'd say some fine gentleman had been taking his pleasure with her, but there's been none such in the village, and Matty's not gone more than half a mile from her home this twelvemonth."

Imelda frowned. "Will the man responsible confess to it?"

"Not if he has Weddon and his sons to reckon with," Abigail said with conviction. "Belike he's wed, too. No, the girl will have to name him."

"And if she refuses to do so?"

"Then 'tis my belief 'twill be the death of her," Abigail replied worriedly. "Weddon won't forgive the disgrace she's brought on him, and he's thrashed her already till she can barely stand. I tried to stop him, for Matty's mother was my cousin and I've a kindness for the girl, but what with him shouting at her to name the man, and preacher standing by calling her whore and Jezebel and I know not what besides, and Matty screaming, and cursing her father as though the Devil was in her, no one paid any heed to me. So I thought I'd best come at once to her ladyship. She's always been kind to Matty, and maybe Squire will speak a word to Weddon."

"I am sure that both Sir Darrell and her ladyship will do all they can to help the girl," Imelda assured her. "I will tell them of it as soon as they return."

She did so, but dusk was falling by the time Charity and Darrell reached the Dower House again, and it was clearly out of the question to visit the Weddon household that night. Next morning, however, Charity made this her first concern, but when she reached the forge a further shock awaited her. Weddon was there, and so was his elder son, Japhet, who worked with him, but when Charity said that she wished to see Matty, the smith shook his head.

"Her be'ant here, m'lady. Her be gone."

"Gone?" Charity repeated blankly. "Gone where?"

Weddon shrugged. "Who's to tell? Slipped out in the night, her did, and naught to tell which way her went."

"Surely you have searched for her?"

The smith looked at her, his heavy, florid face grim and unrelenting. He had left his work when he saw her, and stepped out beneath the low portal of the forge to where she had reined in her horse at the roadside; his reply to her greeting had been properly respectful, but Charity, who had known him since childhood, realized at once that there was no hope of persuading him to forgive his erring daughter.

"I've work to do, m'lady, and no time to waste running hither and yon looking for a slut that's brought disgrace on me. Good riddance, say I! I'd have turned her out anyway once I'd learned whose get the brat is, but since her's gone of her own choice, there's an end to it."

"Weddon, she is your daughter, and only sixteen. Have you no pity?"

"No daughter o' mine now the lying drab!" he replied implacably. "If she'd shown some decent shame, and named the rogue as wronged her, then maybe—!" He shrugged. "But to lie, and say no man's had her, in spite of her swollen belly, and to curse me, her own father, swearing I'd be sorry for giving her the thrashing she deserved—no, m'lady! I be done wi' her."

Nothing Charity could say would shift him from the stand he had taken, and at last she left him and rode on to the inn to take counsel with Abigail Bramble, whose concern for the missing girl she knew to be genuine. Abigail, however, had no counsel to offer.

"Though I be main feared for her, m'lady, and that's the truth," she said anxiously. "Where can she be gone?" She hesitated. "To be honest with you, m'lady, I can't get the thought of the millrace out of my mind."

Charity frowned, for a similar thought had occurred unpleasantly to her. "Suicide? Do you think she would, Abby?"

"She might, being drove to it, poor lass. Wi' no money, and no roof over her head, and a babe coming, she might think 'twere the only way."

"But would she not turn to you, Abby? Or to me? She must know that we would not deny her aid."

Abigail sighed. " 'Tis my belief, m'lady, that the poor wench be crazed. She swore she'd been with no man, for all it's plain to see she's breeding, and the way she screamed and cursed her father when he thrashed her was like a madwoman raving. I've never heard the like in all my days."

"She must be found," Charity said with decision. "She cannot have gone far in so short a time. I will send some of our men to search for her, and ask Mrs. Pennan to do the same, and when they find her she shall come to the Dower House."

"*If* they find her," Mrs. Bramble remarked heavily. "Oh, m'lady, 'tis a bad business, for sure!"

It was to become worse. They had discussed the various places to which Matty's flight might have taken her, and Charity was about to leave, when Abigail's youngest son, Peter, came quickly into the room. He looked white and shocked, and addressed himself abruptly to Charity.

"Will it please you to go back to the forge, m'lady? Weddon's been stricken."

"Stricken?" she repeated sharply. "With what?"

"We can't tell, m'lady." The young man seemed frightened. "He were working at the anvil, then suddenly he staggered and let fall the hammer, and next minute he were stretched out on the ground like one dead. Stricken, that's what he's been!"

Charity went quickly out of the inn and along the village street to the forge, Abigail panting after her. A group of women and one or two old men, with a few small children clinging curiously to the fringe of the crowd, was clustered about the entrance to the smithy, but they drew back immediately to let Lady Conyngton pass. Just within the forge Japhet Weddon knelt, supporting his father in his arms, while two other women tried, apparently without success, to revive the smith. As Charity came in, the younger of the two raised a frightened face towards her.

"Thanks be you've come, m'lady! We can do naught. Look at him."

Charity looked. The big man lay helpless, an inert bulk in the strong arms of his son; the right side of his face was twisted awry and there was a dribble of spittle from the corner of his mouth, but his eyes were open, wide and staring as though in horror at his own plight. His left arm moved convulsively as though he tried to raise himself, but his right, that powerful arm which had swung the heavy hammer and laid a whip about the cringing body of a pregnant girl, trailed like a dead limb on the ground.

"Lord protect us! What ails him?" Abigail's shocked whisper sounded loud in the awed silence, and Charity shook off her own unreasoning alarm and forced herself to speak calmly.

"Whatever it is, he will be better off in his bed than lying upon the ground. Peter Bramble, do you help Japhet to carry his father within. I do not know what affliction had struck him down, but—!"

"Witchcraft!" The harsh voice, speaking just behind

her, made her jump, and she spun round to see the preacher standing on the threshold, a sombre figure against the bright morning. "Can you doubt now, madam, that Satan is abroad in this unhappy place?"

She heard the uneasy murmurs of the onlookers, saw the two women who had been tending the smith rising hastily to their feet, and spoke sharply in an attempt to check the incipient panic, forcing herself to ignore the small, cold prickle of dread along her own nerves.

"Why should witches, if witches there be, turn their malice against this man?"

"Why?" He came farther into the forge. "I marvel, madam, that you need to ask. Did he not chastise one of them, and she his own daughter, and did she not curse him as he did so?"

"Matty? A witch?" Charity spoke with angry scorn. "I'll not believe it."

"Because you will not," he rebuked her harshly. "You are blind, and worse than blind, for out of her own mouth is she convicted. She swears that she has lain with no man, and yet her belly swells with child, and if 'tis not of man's getting then 'tis of the Devil's. She screamed threats and curses at her father when he whipped her, and now the arm that wielded the whip is withered, and he lies helpless, unable to speak or move. This is the work of witches, beyond all doubt."

Charity could find no answer. Her thoughts darted to and fro, seeking one. Everybody knew that witches had the power to harm; to blight crops and cattle, and to torment the bodies of those who had offended them.

Weddon the smith, an hour ago, had been hale and
hearty; now he lay like a living corpse. Abby had
thought Matty Weddon was mad, but what if it were
not so? What if the girl had discovered somehow the
source of some hellish power? Somehow? From whom?
Tabitha Spragge? No, Tabitha was only a senile old
woman. Then where? And how?

And if Matty, who besides? Who else, among these
people whom she had known all her life, were servants
of the Devil? Phrases from one of Dr. Malperne's
sermons flashed into her mind. "It may be that your
neighbour is one such . . . even those closest to you
by ties of blood cannot be above suspicion." If Matty
were indeed a witch, it was unlikely that she practised
her unholy arts alone. It might be that there was a
whole witch coven in Conyngton St. John.

Looking about her, Charity realized that her own
doubts and fears were echoed in the minds of her
companions, for the women were no longer closely
grouped about the doorway. They were edging apart,
looking askance at one another with sidelong glances,
and already she could feel fear and distrust spreading
among them.

Meanwhile the minister was taking charge. At his
direction the two young men lifted the helpless body
of the smith and, staggering a little beneath the weight,
bore it into the small cottage adjoining the forge, while
Malperne turned his attention to the lingering women.

"Go your ways," he admonished them sternly. "Fast
and pray. Seach each one of you her conscience, for
where sinful thoughts intrude, there opens a door to
the powers of evil. And evil is abroad among us this

day in its most frightful guise, the powers of Hell walking alive upon the earth. Go, I say!"

They went, scattering hastily to their homes with scarcely a word one to the other, until only Charity and Abigail were left. Malperne's sombre, burning gaze turned towards them.

"Get you home, my lady, and you, too, Widow Bramble. There is naught for you to do here."

"A physician?" Charity began hesitantly, but he silenced her with an emphatic shake of the head.

"No physician can aid him. Of what avail medicine against the powers of darkness? The witch must be found and imprisoned, and closely watched so that her imps and demons come not to her, for only thus may the spell be broken. She, and any who practise a like abomination, must be found and utterly destroyed, for it is written 'thou shalt not suffer a witch to live.' We must pluck this evil from our midst, purge ourselves of it ere others be stricken as this man was stricken, for great and terrible is the peril in which we stand. The pit yawneth before our feet, and the fires of Hell burn to consume us. Carry that word to your husband, my lady, and bid him mock no more."

He lifted his hand in a gesture which might have been either a warning or a threat, and turned, and stalked like a gaunt black crow into the cottage beyond the forge.

Charity, riding homewards, was more frightened than she had ever been in her life. She knew now that fear had lain at the root of her refusal to believe the preacher's repeated allegations of witchcraft. Fear of learning that he was right, and that there were those among her lifelong friends and neighbours who had pledged themselves to the Devil; fear of the harm they might do; fear of the consequences of a witch-hunt, which must inevitably shatter this little community that, with the exception of her own family, had remained closely united through all the long years of difficulty and hardship.

More than anything she longed to confide her fears to Darrell, to share with him this crisis as they had shared so many others, knowing that to do so would be to find mutual strength and comfort, but Darrell would not be at the Dower House. He had problems weighing upon him far heavier than the mere downfall of a village girl, and he had had no doubt of Charity's ability to deal with a matter as trivial as they had both supposed this to be. He had left that morning for Exeter, intending to spend the next two nights at Sir Richard Linslade's house at Dorringford, a few miles outside the city, and Charity knew that she would have to cope alone with the immediate consequences of what had happened that morning.

She could, of course, send a messenger after him, and there was no doubt that he would return, but not for the world would she lay this extra burden upon him. The business on which he had gone concerned the whole future of their family, even of Conyngton itself, for it was an attempt to raise the money the impoverished estate desperately needed. If he failed, the only alternative would be to sell more land, and there was no doubt which purchaser would outbid his rivals to acquire it. Edward Taynton, on behalf of Mrs. Shenfield, who was still dedicated to her son's design of driving the Conyngtons from their ancestral home.

Charity arrived home in a mood of unwonted pessimism, and looking so grave that Imelda was seriously alarmed. At first Charity was reluctant to speak of what had happened in the village, even though she knew it could not be long before the news reached the Dower House, but the weight of her foreboding was too great to be borne alone. In the end she confided in the girl, thankful that there was someone other than the servants to whom she could talk. They sat together in the parlour, uneasy and uncertain, wondering, with misgiving, what Dr. Malperne was doing.

They were soon to know. During the afternoon Peter Bramble came hastening up the hill to the Dower House in search of Sir Darrell, and was obviously dismayed by the news that the squire was away from home. He stood looking worriedly from one young woman to the other, and reluctantly, prompted by Charity's insistent questions, told them his news.

Malperne, it seemed, had spent a long time at the bedside of the stricken man, wrestling in prayer with the forces of evil, but to no avail. Finally he had come forth and, going about the village, exhorted the men to set out in search of Matty Weddon—"this black witch who by her evil arts hath stricken her father into a living death." The villagers of Conyngton St. John, however, though fearful of witchcraft and now distrustful of one another, yet remained united in their antagonism towards Malperne. If the squire told them to search for Matty they would do it, but not one of them would stir a step at the bidding of the Puritan preacher they hated and despised.

"So then he abused us very hotly, calling us cowards and worse, and saying as there were some not yet so lost to their Christian duty as to let a witch go unsought and unpunished, and he set off towards the Moat House. I followed, thinking it best to learn what he intended. I dursn't go nigh the house, but I hid myself in sight of it, and after a time he came out again, and most o' the servants, women as well as men, with him."

Charity was frowning. "To search for Matty?"

"I couldn't tell, m'lady," Peter admitted, looking perplexed. "If that was their purpose, you'd think they'd scatter, but all went off in a mob towards the village, wi' preacher leading 'em. I thought then, Squire 'd best be told, for there'll likely be trouble 'tween them and our own folk, things being as they are."

Charity agreed. There was no love lost between the villagers and the servants of the Moat House, most of whom were "foreigners" from Plymouth or even farther afield. There had been minor clashes between individuals in the past; if Mrs. Shenfield's people were going in a body to the village, already tense and uneasy after the events of the past twenty-four hours, a pitched battle might well develop.

"How long since?" she asked Peter.

"Maybe half an hour, my lady. I had to bide hid, you see, for there was others coming from the fields to join the house servants."

"Cousin!" Imelda spoke urgently as a thought occurred to her. "Is it possible that Dr. Malperne was leading them to old Tabitha's cottage? She has been named 'witch,' and he may think to find Matty there, or that the old woman knows where she is hidden."

"It is very likely!" Charity sprang to her feet. "Send for my horse, Imelda, and bid them hasten. Whether at Tabitha's or elsewhere, Malperne will be stirring up trouble, you may depend. Peter, start back towards the village. I will overtake you."

Imelda was dismayed, but she had been long enough at the Dower House to know that it would be useless to argue. With Sir Darrell absent, Charity would not hesitate to do what she knew he would do in such circumstances, which was to use every endeavour to prevent the situation from becoming out of hand. So she ran to give the orders, telling the servants to saddle not one horse, but two, with two mounted grooms to attend her ladyship. Then she hurried to fetch Charity's hat, and her own hood and cloak.

"I am coming with you, cousin," she announced, seeing Charity's frowning glance, and added quickly: "Sir Darrell would not wish you to go alone."

"Sir Darrell would not wish either of us to go," Charity retorted with a flash of wry humour. "Come, then, and"—she paused for an instant to lay a hand on Imelda's arm—"thank you, my dear."

They overtook Peter Bramble near the foot of the hill, and he turned an anxious glance up towards Charity as she drew rein for a moment beside him.

"Miss Imelda were right, m'lady. They be at Tabby's sure enough—I can hear shouting over yonder."

She nodded and spurred forward again, Imelda and the grooms pounding after her. Tabitha's cottage was on the outskirts of the village, a tumbledown ruin of a place standing somewhat apart from its neighbours and separated from them by a straggling spinney which hid it from Charity and her companions as they galloped towards it, but from behind the trees came a confused clamour of voices, shouts and cries which were unintelligible yet somehow menacing. Then, as they rounded the end of the spinney and came in sight of the cottage and the crowd milling before it, there rose above all other sounds a thin, high screaming, chilling and scarcely human, which ceased as suddenly as it had begun. . . .

At the sight of the horses bearing down upon them the crowd parted involuntarily, in a mad scramble to avoid the plunging hooves, and the four riders dashed between them to the very door of the cottage, where stood Dr. Malperne and one or two hardier spirits who had stood their ground. Old Tabitha lay huddled on the ground at their feet. They had stripped her naked, and her scrawny, wrinkled body, repulsive as that of a newly hatched bird, was bruised and bleeding in a dozen places, while a heavier flow of blood stained her sparse white hair.

Charity's horse was brought to plunging halt beside the little group and she took in the scene before her with eyes blazing with anger. She forgot that the old woman might well be a witch, a servant of the powers of darkness, and that Malperne stood for Parliament as well as for the Puritan faith, and had the confidence of Mrs. Shenfield and the influential Edward Taynton. All that mattered was that one of Darrell's people—

her people—had been set upon and dragged from her home and mercilessly ill used.

"What means this?" she demanded of Malperne, and it was as though she spoke to an impertinent lackey. "Is this how you do the Christian duty you prate of, by mishandling the old and defenceless?"

A dark flush of mortification rose in the preacher's gaunt cheeks at her tone. "The hag is a foul witch," he said harshly. "We seek the young one, or news of her, and where better to search than here, where we might be sure of laying by the heels at least one of the Devil's minions."

"*You* say she is a witch."

"It is proven, madam. She bears the witch-mark on her foul body."

A contemptuous gesture indicated the naked, bleeding figure at his feet, and as Charity looked again at the mob's victim, her anger broke from the last shred of control.

"And if she bears it ten times over, you and this rabble you have raised are not judge and jury. Take them back whence they came, where they belong. This is Conyngton land, and I will have no lackeys from the Moat House rioting here."

Malperne stood his ground, glaring up at her, and so did the little group around him, while the rest, seeing that Lady Conyngton was accompanied only by another woman and two grooms, clowed in about them. Imelda, who had felt she could not bear the sight of Tabitha's crumpled, pathetic nakedness, had slipped from the saddle while Charity was speaking to spread her cloak over the old woman. Now the forward surge of the crowd separated her from her companions and forced her closer to the group about the cottage door; she found herself within a yard of Daniel Stotewood, and shuddered, but he seemed unaware of her existence. He stood with folded arms, staring at Charity; staring as though he saw no one else at all, with a look of such concentrated venom in his pale eyes that Imelda knew with chilling certainty that if he were indeed crazed, his madness took the form of a hatred of Lady Conyngton which was almost murderous.

"Have a care, my lady," Malperne was grimly warning Charity. "To traffic with witches is almost as grave a sin as to practise witchcraft itself, and to defend one is to set one's feet on the path to eternal damnation. Tabitha Spragge is a notorious witch, who has doubtless led Matilda Weddon into the worship and service of the foul Fiend, and she shall be made to reveal the girl's hiding place."

A roar of agreement from his followers applauded and confirmed his words, and they began to press even closer about Lady Conyngton and her servants. One of them even went so far as to lay a hand on the bridle of Charity's black mare, only to recoil with a howl of pain as her riding-whip slashed fiercely across his arm. With that small incident came a subtle change in the demeanour of the crowd; their attitude was now actively menacing, and though the two grooms drew protectively closer to their mistress, it was plain that they could have little hope of defending her against a concerted attack. As for Imelda, dismounted and separated from her companions, she would be entirely at the mercy of the mob. Fists were shaken, stout cudgels brandished threateningly. Malperne, who might have restrained them, made no attempt to do so, and Daniel Stotewood stood silent and motionless, still staring fixedly at the tall, dark woman on the black mare.

Imelda, cowering against the wall of the cottage, jostled and buffeted, became aware of a drumming sound which at first seemed no louder than the frightened thudding of her own heart, but which, after a moment, she recognized as the beat of rapidly approaching hooves. Was help coming, and if so, from whom? Sir Darrell, unexpectedly returned? She could think of no other possibility.

The rider swept into view from beyond the spinney, bringing with him a flash of scarlet, and the glint of sunlight on helmet and breastplate of polished steel. Imelda gasped, and closed her eyes for an instant, almost believing that her present peril had evoked the memory of an earlier danger, and a vision of the man who had saved her from it. Yet when she looked again he was still there, mounted on the chestnut stallion, towering above the crowd which was only just becoming aware of his arrival.

"Hold, there!" The deep, remembered voice, with its note of authority and command, rang like a trumpet-call above the shouts and jeers, so that hubbub dwindled raggedly towards silence. "Quit this unseemly brawling, and let me pass."

They obeyed, falling back in so haphazard a fashion that they jostled and stumbled one over the other. He was one man against a score, but his air of command,

and the authority of the uniform he wore, wrought
upon them to a degree which to Imelda seemed little
short of miraculous. A pathway opened before him
of its own accord to the very threshold of the cottage,
and with the exception of Stotewood, even those who
had stood there with the minister sought to slink off
to join their fellows.

Giles rode forward, saluted Lady Conyngton and
sent one swift, reassuring glance at Imelda where she
stood backed against the wall. Then he was curtly
addressing Malperne.

"You sir, appear to be the leader of this mob. What
make you here?"

The preacher flushed again at the abrupt demand,
but, voiced by an officer of the New Model, it was a
very different matter from a similar question asked
a few minutes earlier by a mere woman, and she the
wife of a noted malignant. Ungraciously he explained.
There was ample evidence of witchcraft in the village;
a man had been stricken almost to death, and that,
it seemed, by his own daughter; the old woman was a
notorious witch, and so—

"And so you lead a rabble here to hunt and torture,"
Giles cut in sternly. "If the woman be suspect, she
should be taken before the Justices and accused in
proper form, so that a just inquiry into the charge
may be made. That, sir, were your duty. That, and
no more."

"Time presses," Malperne replied angrily. "The
young witch had disappeared, and must be found if
her father is to be released from her foul enchant-

ments. It is likely that this hag knows where she has concealed herself."

"And if she does, do you think to discover it by beating her insensible?" Giles took a second look at the crumpled figure beneath the cloak, and frowned. Then he swung abruptly from the saddle, tossing the reins to one of Charity's attendants, and bent for a few moments over Tabitha. When he straightened up again his face was very stern, and his eyes as cold as ice. "The woman is dead."

Malperne looked taken aback, and a ripple of uneasiness passed over his followers, for this was something they had not bargained for. After a pause the preacher said sullenly:

"That was not intended."

"Intended or not, the fact remains. Murder has been done here this day."

"Murder?" Malperne was angry again. "Of a foul witch, a servant and worshipper of the Devil?"

"So *you* say. The charge had not been proved." Giles was very quiet, in marked contrast to the minister's hectoring tone. "Mark you, sir, there will be an accounting demanded of this day's work, for what you and these others have done is beyond the law. And let me not hear of similar violence towards the young woman when you find her. Take her at once before the Justices and make formal accusation against her."

Malperne cast a quick look around him. Already, from the edges of the crowd, some of the Moat House servants were beginning to slip away, to edge furtively out of the sight of this stern young officer and then to take to their heels. The minister saw his authority slipping away with them, and spoke belligerently in an effort to recapture it.

"Who *are* you, sir, and by what right do you lay your commands upon us?"

"I am Major Bradwell of the Plymouth garrison, and it is my duty, among other things, to ensure that order is maintained in the countryside. Which it will not be, sir, if men like you, ministers of the Word with authority among your fellows, set the law at naught with rabble-raising and witch-hunts." He glanced at Daniel Stotewood, and gestured imperiously towards Tabitha's body. "You fellow! Carry this poor creature within until order may be taken for her burial, while the rest of you," his gaze swept sternly over the hang-dog remnants of the crowd, "get you to your homes, and think well on what you have done this day."

In silence they obeyed him, sobered by the knowledge of an old woman brutally done to death, and yet Imelda had an uneasy feeling that the violence had been only temporarily curbed. Giles Bradwell represented the authority of the army, an authority they did not dare to defy, but the fear and hatred of witches lurked still beneath the surface, and might well erupt again once his restraining presence was withdrawn. She had had her first experience that day of the power of a mob, and it had left her shaken and afraid.

Giles did not wait to see the last of the crowd, but beckoned forward the groom who held the bridle of Imelda's horse. Then he turned to her where she still stood with her back against the cottage wall; he did not speak, just looked for a brief, intent moment into her eyes, and then set his hands about her waist and with one easy movement lifted her into the saddle, turning to his own mount before she could even utter an incoherent murmur of thanks. In some confusion, conscious of Charity watching them, she bent forward to arrange her skirts, hoping thus to hide the colour she felt rising in her cheeks.

Giles mounted, and with Charity on one side and Imelda on the other, and the grooms bringing up the rear, turned in the direction of the Dower House. From the threshold of the dead woman's cottage Dr. Malperne and Daniel Stotewood, standing together and yet each, in some indefinable way, totally isolated from the other, watched them go.

"You place us even deeper in your debt, Major Bradwell," Charity said as they passed the spinney, "though I am perplexed to know how you happened to arrive just when we stood in need of help."

"My duties had taken me towards Exeter, madam," he replied, "and since I was returning within a mile or two of Conyngton St. John, it occurred to me to pay my respects to Sir Darrell and your ladyship. When I reached the Dower House I found your servants in great anxiety on your behalf, and when I heard what they had to tell, it seemed to me that they had good cause. I came after you, and as I rode down the hill I met a young man hastening up it, who, when I questioned him, told me what was afoot here, and that he was on his way to summon the rest of your servants to your aid. I told him to stay where he was while I followed you myself—aye, and there he is!"

Peter Bramble, hesitating in desperate uncertainty at the roadside, came forward at a run to meet them.

"Be all well, m'lady?"

"All is well with us, Peter, thanks to Major Bradwell," she replied gravely, "but Tabitha is dead."

"And Matty Weddon, m'lady?"

Charity shook her head. "No sign of her. If Tabitha knew aught, she died before she could disclose it."

"Go back to the village," Giles said abruptly, "and make it known there that if the girl is found, she must not be harmed, but taken immediately before the Justices. There must be no searching for witch-marks, no prickings or swimmings to learn whether or no she be guilty. That will be for her judges to determine."

Peter looked at Charity for guidance as to whether or not he should obey, but when she nodded, he touched his forelock and turned away, while the others rode slowly up the hill. Giles, who so far had heard only a garbled version of what had occurred, sought enlightenment, and Charity described to him the events of the past two days.

Imelda, riding silently beside them, could only be thankful that Lady Conyngton held his attention. She had thought of him so often; dreamed, without hope, of meeting him again, that now the seemingly impossible had happened she was overcome by self-consciousness. Questions teased at her mind. Why had he come? Courtesy had not demanded so much of him that he should ride several miles out of his way merely to pay his respects to people he scarcely knew, and who were of political and religious beliefs totally opposed to his own. Was it possible that he had come to see *her*? And if he had, what good would come of it, for either of them?

When they reached the Dower House, where the servants greeted Lady Conyngton with undisguised relief, he accepted an invitation to enter and take some refreshment. Imelda had paid very little heed to the conversation as they rode up the hill, being fully occupied with her own thoughts, but she had the impression that Giles had said very little. Once they were alone in the parlour, however, and a servant had brought ale for him and wine for Charity and herself, he said abruptly:

"My lady, I did not wish to delve too deeply into the matter before your grooms, but that crowd I dispersed—they came not from the village?"

"No, Major Bradwell, from the Moat House. The servants there are nearly all strangers in Conyngton St. John. Foreigners, the villagers call them."

"And your minister found it necessary to call upon these to seek out witches?" There was a hint of sternness in Giles's voice. "These, and no others?"

Charity's dark eyes regarded him steadily. "The Conyngtons, Major, as I am sure you must know, remain loyal to the King and to the Church of England, and the villagers hold like loyalties. They are as shocked and frightened as I by what happened this morning, by this evidence that Dr. Malperne is right when he speaks of witches here, but they will make no move at his bidding. The Moat House is a Puritan household and its members obey him readily enough."

"The more readily, perhaps, when it may mean a clash with the village people?" Giles suggested shrewdly. Charity made a little gesture of dissent, and he added with a slight smile: "Have no fear, madam. I am not trying to trap you into admissions harmful to your family or to your tenants."

For a moment or two she continued to look searchingly at him; he sustained the gaze calmly, and after a little she smiled, rather wryly.

"I ask your pardon, Major Bradwell. These are uneasy times, and one learns caution perforce. Moreover, the differences between the Conyngtons and the Shenfields of the Moat House are more immediate and personal than those of politics and religion." She stopped abruptly, looked from one to the other of her companions, and then got up from her chair. "Forgive me—these matters are too painful for me to speak of. Miss Hallett will explain to you what I mean."

She went out, so quickly that Imelda scarcely realized what was happening until she found herself alone with Giles. She was astonished by Charity's behaviour, for she knew by now the other woman's strength of character, and though it could not be pleasant to explain family differences to a stranger, it was not like Charity to shrink from an unpleasant necessity. She had no chance to pursue the thought, however, since Giles was waiting for the promised explanation.

"The Shenfields are Lady Conyngton's own family," she said baldly, in answer to his puzzled look, "and it was her cousin, Jonas Shenfield, who led the troop that burned the manor house."

Briefly she outlined the story Charity had told her, speaking hurriedly and not looking at him as she talked, while Giles watched her, and wondered if he had been a fool to come. He had tried to resist the temptation: had fought against it until the very moment he reached the crossroads where he must turn aside to visit Conyngton St. John, but in the end he had succumbed, and for what? It was true that he had been of some service to her and to Lady Conyngton, for the situation outside the witch's cottage had looked uncommonly ugly when he arrived, but since then she had not spoken, had scarcely even looked at him until Lady Conyngton's withdrawal compelled her to acknowledge his presence. She seemed as remote and unfriendly as she had at their first meeting.

He began to feel angry with her and with himself, for the feelings she aroused were a complication in his life which he had neither expected nor desired. He was ambitious; he had prospered in his chosen profession, and aimed to climb higher yet; in time he would marry, choosing, as the custom was, a bride whose fortune and family connections would further his career, for sentiment had no place in the serious business of choosing a wife and ensuring the continued prosperity of one's family.

Then she had come, this slim, brown girl, and in a few short hours had taken such possession of his heart that, try as he would, he could not drive her from it. His mind might reiterate his folly, telling him that there could be no common meeting-ground for an officer of the New Model Army and the daughter of impoverished Royalist gentlefolk; that her family would undoubtedly condemn such a union as bitterly as his own; that he should put Imelda Hallett from his thoughts and make no attempts to see her again, but he had paid no heed to the promptings of common sense. An opportunity had arisen and he had taken it, and now he was well served for his folly. She was not even glad to see him again.

In spite of the turmoil of his feelings, another part of his mind was taking in the story she was telling him, of old wrongs and enduring hatred, and he perceived that there was another danger here, quite apart from the actual horrors of witchcraft.

"When I was here before," he said bluntly when the story was ended, "Sir Darrell Conyngton scorned the warning the preacher brought, of witches in this parish, and today her ladyship sought to protect a woman so accused. They should curb such rashness, and move against the evil as the law requires."

She did look at him then, her expression puzzled and slightly indignant. "*You* condemned Dr. Malperne and his followers for what they had done."

"I condemned them for taking the law into their own hands, that is all. Witchcraft is the foulest of all crimes, and it is the clear duty of every man—and every woman—to seek out those who practise such abomination and to hand them over to the law. Remind Sir Darrell of that when he returns."

"*I* remind him? I can imagine how he would receive such an impertinence."

"Then tell him that you speak for me."

Imelda flushed scarlet. Was he making game of her,

or implying—what was he implying? Speak for him, indeed! She said indignantly:

"It were far better, sir, for you to speak for yourself. Put your commands in writing, and I will undertake to see that Sir Darrell receives them the instant he returns. Wait! I will fetch pen and paper."

She went quickly towards the door, but Giles's long stride took him to it before her, and his hand closed on her arm as she reached for the handle. She tried to jerk away, but with as little success as if she had tried to free herself from an iron manacle. He looked down at her flushed, angry face, and his own was very stern.

"This is not a game, Miss Hallett, and I do not command. I advise. You say that Mrs. Shenfield bears a grudge against Sir Darrell and his lady. What do you suppose would happen if she informed the authorities in Plymouth that they offer succour and comfort to witches?"

The quietly spoken question drove all thought of herself from Imelda's mind, and anger and embarrassment alike perished in a cold tide of fear. She remembered that Ellen Shenfield had given Charity a similar warning, and she recalled, too, the elder Mrs. Shenfield's hard, uncompromising face and implacable eyes. The woman did cherish an undying enmity towards the Conyngtons, and by now her servants would have carried word to her of Charity's defence of Tabitha Spragge. Dr. Malperne, too, would not readily forgive the tone which had been taken with him.

Giles saw the paling of her cheeks, and the alarm that came leaping into her eyes, and his own eyes narrowed. "Has there already been some talk of this?"

"A little." She told him what she knew. "But there is no truth in it. At first they could not believe such evil of their own people, but what happened this morning convinced Lady Conyngton that Dr. Malperne is right. Then we heard that he had called out the servants from the Moat House, and she went to try to prevent trouble between them and the villagers, but when she saw what they had done to old Tabitha, she lost her temper." She looked pleadingly up at him. "You were angry yourself."

"Yes." A slight smile relaxed the sternness of his expression for a moment before he continued gravely: "It is an ill thing when a mob takes the law into its own hands, no matter what the cause. A thing easier to start than to halt, as Dr. Malperne learned today."

"He did not even attempt to halt it," Imelda said in a low voice. "He just stood there and watched— and so did Daniel Stotewood."

"Who is Daniel Stotewood?"

"One of the Moat House servants. He whom you ordered to carry Tabitha's body within. He hates Lady Conyngton."

"Why?"

"I do not know. I think he must be crazed, for he watches her all the time as though he sees no one else, and can think of nothing but his hatred of her. He would have been glad today to see her used as they used Tabitha Spragge." Her glance lifted again to meet his challengingly this time. "You think that fanciful, but I know that what I say is true."

"I think you have not yet recovered from your

fright," he replied reassuringly. "The fellow may nurse some grudge against her ladyship, but a servant's spite is of small account. Mrs. Shenfield and the minister are a different matter, and I counsel you most strongly to tell Sir Darrell what I have said. Or tell her ladyship, so that she may pass on the warning."

Imelda answered somewhat at random, for suddenly she was no longer thinking entirely of either danger escaped or danger threatened. Giles's bruising grip on her arm had long since relaxed, but now his hand was clasped lightly about hers. She was not quite sure how this had happened, and she knew she ought not to permit it, yet she made no attempt to draw her hand away. She felt too shy to look up again, for she somehow knew that he was watching her intently.

"Is all well with you?" he asked softly. "I have often wondered—are you happy here?"

Imelda's heart gave a little leap of delight. So he had been thinking of her, as she had been thinking of him. She nodded.

"Very happy," she murmured. "Lady Conyngton could not be kinder. Sir Darrell, too."

"And did your servant recover from his injuries?"

"Yes, and went home to Wiltshire. My parents were much shocked to hear of what had happened, and my father wrote a letter charging me, should I ever chance to meet with you again, to express their gratitude for what you did. They would have cause to thank you again today."

He brushed this aside. "It was my happiness, then as now, to serve you." He hesitated, and then added in a lower tone: "As it will always be."

She was startled into looking up. The serious, blue-grey eyes were still intently regarding her; there seemed to be an unspoken question in that steady gaze, and her own eyes must have answered it, for suddenly he smiled and his fingers tightened for a instant upon hers, though all he said was:

"It grows late. I must find her ladyship and take leave of her. God's blessing on you."

He held her hand to his lips for a moment, and then he was gone. As she had done once before, Imelda stood listening to his footsteps going away from her, but this time the sound brought no sense of desolation; this time she knew he would return.

He came again sooner than she had expected or even dared to hope, riding up the hill from the village a bare ten days after his previous visit. They were days in which a good deal had happened. Imelda had faithfully recounted to Charity what Giles had said to her about Mrs. Shenfield, and she had no doubt that Charity had passed the warning on to Darrell as soon as he returned from Exeter.

He had at once caused a search to be made for Matty Weddon, but though the villagers sought her in every likely spot they met with no more success than had the servants from the Moat House a few days earlier. The girl had disappeared as completely as though she had vanished into thin air, and there were not a few people who believed she had done just that, or else invoked that other well-known power of witches, and transformed herself into a hare or other commonplace animal in order to evade detection.

Meanwhile her father still lay helpless, the whole right side of his body powerless, and his mouth so deadened and twisted that he could utter only unintelligible sounds.

Within a week of Tabitha Spragge's death, Dr. Malperne had been summoned to Plymouth, to answer, so it was said, to the Justices for the part he had played in the old woman's murder. In spite of the dread of witchcraft which now had the whole parish in its grip, there were many who hoped that he would never return.

Sir Darrell had come home from Exeter with his financial difficulties still unsolved. Imelda naturally knew nothing of these, but she sensed that there was something amiss which had nothing whatsoever to do with recent events in Conyngton St. John. The lines which old sorrows and present care had etched in Darrell's face seemed more deeply graven, and now and then, in an unguarded moment worry and trouble looked out of Charity's dark eyes. Imelda, already deeply attached to them both, wondered anxiously what was wrong, and wished that it lay in her power to help.

On the day that Giles Bradwell came again to the Dower House she was returning from an errand to one of the neighbouring farms. For the most part her way had lain by wood and meadow, but near the Dower House she had to follow the road from the village, and it was here that Giles overtook her. At the first sound of approaching hoof-beats she felt a flicker of apprehension, and cast a quick glance over her shoulder, but one glimpse of the familiar chestnut horse and tall, scarlet-coated rider allayed her momentary alarm, replacing it with a rush of gladness and excitement which took her unawares. She stopped and waited for him, with flushed cheeks and shining eyes, and when he dismounted beside her, stretched out her hand to him in an unselfconscious gesture of welcome.

He took the slight fingers and kissed them as though he would have preferred to kiss her lips, and then for a few moments they stood handfasted, just looking at each other in a silence that somehow said things they did not yet dare to put into words. When at last they spoke, it was in polite and formal phrases that had nothing whatsoever to do with what their eyes had been soundlessly saying.

"Good-day to you, Major Bradwell. We did not look to see you again in Conyngton so soon."

"Nor I to be here, Miss Hallett, but certain matters have arisen in Plymouth which I think Sir Darrell should know. I trust he is not still from home?"

"Oh, no! He returned nearly a week ago, and I believe you will find him now at the Dower House."

"Are you on your way home? May I walk with you?"

She assented, and they went together up the hill at the slowest possible pace, for they both knew, without consciously thinking about it, that their meeting was a stroke of good fortune which would probably never occur again. They spoke little, and then only to exchange a few commonplace remarks, and yet the silence between them was still more eloquent than words.

The road stretched before them, patched with sunlight and shadow; their feet, and the horses's hooves, raised little clouds of pinkish-brown dust from its surface; they were enveloped in sudden perfume from a hawthorn tree in full bloom. Imelda was filled with a happiness such as she had never known. She glanced up at the tall young man beside her, and now she no longer saw the hated scarlet and steel of an enemy army, but only the strong, sensitive face and the look in the serious, blue-grey eyes. He smiled at her, and reached for her hand again, so that they passed through the gateway leading to the Dower House with their fingers once more entwined.

Beyond the gate they entered the shade of the long, narrow belt of woodland which shielded house and gardens from the road, and in the very heart of it, where the track curved sharply between great clumps of holly trees, they suddenly came face to face with Rebecca Moone. Coming so abruptly and unexpectedly upon her, it seemed to Imelda almost as though the woman had materialized like a malevolent spirit, and the shock jerked a little, gasping cry from her lips. Then she stood frozen, unable to speak or move, for, taken unawares, she had had no chance to avoid Rebecca's eyes, and now the strange, bright gaze held hers and she was gripped by abject terror and an overpowering sense of evil. She was utterly alone, in cold and darkness, defenceless before some nameless horror.

Giles's horse, startled by the encounter, had snorted and shied, so that he was obliged to let go Imelda's hand to control and quieten it. For a second or two Rebecca stood motionless in the middle of the way, and then she averted her face, sketched a quick curtsy, and moved silently to vanish among the trees on the far side of the track.

Imelda found herself trembling violently, shivering as though the summer day had suddenly been transmuted into bitterest winter. She heard Giles's exclamation of concern and turned blindly towards him, clutching his arm with both hands and burying her face against his sleeve, while he, his other hand fully occupied in restraining the still uneasy horse, looked helplessly down at her. With the warmth of human contact the horror and the darkness were gradually dispelled, and reality swam back into focus; she released his arm and stepped back, her cheeks flaming scarlet, for her mood of idyllic happiness had been rudely shattered, and now everything seemed ordinary and commonplace again.

"Forgive me," she stammered. "I was foolish—she startled me, appearing so suddenly. I did not know—"

The words trailed lamely into silence and she glanced uneasily toward the place where Rebecca had disappeared among the trees. The branches, thick with glossy, sharp-spiked leaves, looked like an impenetrable wall. Could anything have passed through it? Anything human?

Almost as the thought entered her mind she was chiding herself for it, condemning such fanciful nonsense. Rebecca was undeniably human, and she was constantly roaming the countryside in search of plants for her distilling, so that she must know every path that threaded it and could pass where others would suppose it impossible to go. The only real cause for disquiet lay in the fact that the woman had seen Imelda strolling hand-in-hand with Major Bradwell, and might, out of sheer malice, carry the tale to Lady Conyngton.

Giles himself, still mechanically soothing his nervous horse, watched Imelda with perplexity and lingering concern. Even he had been startled by their sudden encounter with the woman with the hideously scarred features, but the girl's reaction was out of all proportion to the incident. Her face had been so drained of colour that he thought she was about to faint, and while she clung to his arm he had been aware of the violence of her trembling.

"Do you know the woman?" he asked after a moment.

"Oh, yes. She is Lady Conyngton's stillroom maid, Rebecca Moone."

"She is grievously afflicted."

"Yes." Imelda began to walk on, quickly now, for she was anxious to be out of the gloom of the woodland. "She dislikes being seen by strangers, which is why she hurried away."

Giles was silent until they reached the edge of the wood and felt again the warmth of the sun. Then he halted and set his free hand on Imelda's shoulder, turning her to face him.

"Why are you afraid of her?" he asked quietly. "Is it just her looks, or is there some other reason?" He paused, but when she did not reply, added gently: "There is no shame, you know, in being repelled by an unpleasant sight."

Imelda turned her face away from that too perceptive gaze, for not even to him could she speak of the real cause of her fear of Rebecca Moone, or of the horror which for an instant in the wood had brushed her with cold, dark wings. That had been mere fancy, anyway; it must have been born of shock and dismay and perhaps a little, too, of guilt.

"I told you, she startled me, appearing without warning. That is all."

"Is it?" There was a wry note in his voice. "Well, I cannot compel you to confide in me, more's the pity." He was silent for a moment, and then asked an unexpected question. "Do you often walk alone, as you were doing when we met?"

"If need be, when, as today, I go upon some errand for Lady Conyngton. Is there any reason why I should not?" Surprise had made her look at him again, and, seeing the frown in his eyes, she repeated, less certainly: "Is there?"

"Perhaps. The whole neighbourhood is restless and uneasy in its fear of witches, and matters may grow worse before all is done. Fear breeds violence, and one never knows when or where it may erupt." He hesitated, still frowning, and then added seriously: "I have no right, I know, to ask it of you, but will you promise me not to walk abroad again unattended?"

At this evidence of his concern for her, Imelda's heart began to beat joyously fast, so that her voice when she replied was breathless and uneven. She looked trustfully up into his face, the thought of dissimulation never entering her head.

"Of course," she said simply, "if that is what you wish."

There was a little silence as they stood looking at

each other. Behind them, a breeze sighed through the wood, and a couple of hundred yards away the Dower House drowsed in the sunshine amid its old-fashioned garden, its windows twinkling like kindly eyes. And eyes might well be watching, Giles remembered, their attention caught by the brightness of a scarlet coat and an apricot-coloured gown against the green of grass and trees; perhaps even the eyes of Sir Darrell Conyngton himself, who would certainly not look with favour on the sight. For Imelda's sake this delightful interlude must be prolonged no further.

"Thank you," he said quietly. "I trust there will be no more lawlessness of the kind I interrupted last time I rode this way, but it is wiser to take no risks."

He was still grasping her lightly by the shoulder. He allowed his hand to slide gently down to her waist, and lifted it, and once more pressed a kiss upon her fingers. For a fleeting moment they clung to his, and then, as though she, too, had remembered the watchful house, were softly withdrawn as she turned to walk sedately on along the track.

As Giles had suspected, they were being observed, though not by Sir Darrell, and not from the house. Charity, walking in the garden with Roxanne, had seen with some dismay that flash of colour at the woodland's edge. So Giles Bradwell was here again, and there could be little doubt of the lure which brought him, or how gladly he must have been welcomed. Imelda's feelings had been transparently plain to her from the very first, and she had also perceived, on the day he rescued them from the witch-hunters, Giles's real reason for returning to Conyngton St. John.

Out of sympathy, and gratitude for the service he had rendered them, she had yielded to a kindly impulse and left him alone with Imelda, though she had later had serious misgivings as to the wisdom of what she had done. She had grown fond of Imelda, and, knowing from her own experience just what it meant to love a man whose political and religious beliefs were in direct opposition to those of one's guardian, could see only heartache ahead for the girl. Now, seeing them together by the wood, she realized with a twinge of conscience that it would have been a greater kindness, to both of them, if she had firmly checked the affair at the outset.

When she saw them walking towards the house, she discreetly steered her companion in the same direction, so that they met Imelda and Giles at the door. She obligingly accepted the explanation that Major Bradwell had business with Sir Darrell, and having presented him to the intrigued and curious Roxanne, left the two younger women together while she took him to find her husband.

Darrell was in a small room at the south-east corner of the house, frowning over account-books which could not be persuaded to tell anything but a discouraging tale. He looked surprised and not altogether pleased when Charity entered with Giles Bradwell, but he greeted the Major courteously, and expressed his sense of obligation for the rescue of his wife and cousin from Malperne's witch-hunt.

Giles shook his head. "I am glad, Sir Darrell, that I chanced to be here when my presence was of some service to her ladyship and Miss Hallett. I have no sympathy with those who raise and let loose a mob to serve their own ends, no matter how worthy those ends may be. That is why I am here."

He glanced from one to the other. "You know that Dr. Malperne was lately summoned to Plymouth to give account of his part in the death of the old woman, Tabitha Spragge?"

"We know that he has gone to Plymouth, and we guessed the cause," Darrell agreed. "Well, Major?"

"He answered the charge against him with accusations of his own. He said that he had been obliged to call upon Mrs. Shenfield's servants for help in seeking out the witches since neither you, Sir Darrell, nor any of your people, would make any move against them."

"That is untrue!" Charity said indignantly. "My husband was not even in Conyngton St. John when Matty Weddon disappeared, but I had a search made for her."

"Dr. Malperne declares that he has given warning of the peril time and again from the pulpit, as well as coming here to seek help, but all in vain. He even had the impertinence to call upon me to confirm the story of one such visit."

"Impertinence, sir?" There was a hint of challenge in Darrell's quiet, stern voice. "I must confess that your choice of words surprise me."

"Yet it need not, Sir Darrell," Giles replied frankly. "I am a soldier, and I see the army in which I serve bedevilled by fanaticism of the sort your preacher displays. I dislike being made a party to it. It sometimes seems to me that when the discovery of witches rests in the hands of such as Dr. Malperne the hunt spawns an evil almost as great as that which it seeks to destroy."

Charity nodded silent agreement, remembering Tabitha's pitiful corpse, and the threats and jeers of the mob, while Darrell studied the soldier with a new interest.

"Such sentiments, sir, do you honour, and are not those I would have expected to hear from one of your persuasion," he said bluntly. "I believe, though, that you could not deny having seen Malperne here, or that he warned you against witchcraft."

"True, Sir Darrell," Giles agreed dryly, "but I did not hear *you* scoff at the warning, or refuse to act upon it. You may be sure I made that plain to those who questioned me, so in the end he gained nothing by calling upon me for support."

"Then wherein lies the harm?" Charity asked in a puzzled tone. "I can well believe that Malperne will try to stir up trouble for us in Plymouth, but will he succeed?"

"Unaided, perhaps not," Giles replied gravely, "but though I failed him, he has since found an ally. One Edward Taynton, a citizen of some considerable standing in the town." He saw his companions exchange glances and added: "That does not surprise you?"

"It does not," Darrell assented grimly. "Taynton is son-in-law to Mrs. Shenfield, and has little cause to love us."

"And Mrs. Jonas Shenfield has already warned her ladyship on this score," Giles said thoughtfully, adding in explanation as he saw their startled looks: "Miss Hallett told me, on the day Tabitha Spragge was killed." He was silent for a moment, frowning. "Malperne, and Mrs. Shenfield, and now Mr. Taynton! Considerable forces are being arrayed against you, Sir Darrell, and you would do well to consider what measures to take against them should the need arise. Is there still no trace of the other suspected witch?"

"No, none." Darrell spoke rather curtly, for though he believed that Bradwell's warning was well intentioned, it galled him be given advice by one whom he could not regard as other than an enemy. "I begin to think there never will be. If she is not dead by now, she must have fled into the Moor, which amounts to the same thing."

"At least no one else had been afflicted," Charity said hopefully. "Perhaps Tabitha had indeed turned from white magic to black, and had led Matty Weddon along the same evil path, but now that the one is dead, and the other vanished, it may be that the evil had spent itself."

"It is my devout hope, madam, that you are right," Giles agreed, though he did not believe that she was. Dr. Malperne was possessed by a burning conviction that his parish was infested with witches whom it was his mission to detect and destroy; he would not rest content until the missing girl was found. Edward Taynton was bent upon causing trouble for the Conyngtons, and Mrs. Shenfield bore them an undying grudge; and trouble for the Conyngtons meant also trouble for Imelda. . . .

He wondered if there was anything he could do to

avert it, except to keep a watchful eye on events in Plymouth and be ready to act at once should the need arise. It was plain that neither he nor his warning was really welcome at the Dower House, at least as far as the master of the house was concerned. Conyngton was courteous, even occasionally cordial, but Giles could see how he resented the need for it; but Sir Darrell, presumably, had never seen a witch-hunt. Giles had, years before in the northern counties, and battle-hardened soldier though he now was, the memory of it haunted him yet. He could only hope that Sir Darrell would not have similar memories to haunt him in the years to come.

Realizing that for the present he could do no more, he rose to take his leave, only to find that the punctilious Conyngton courtesy towards a guest, even an uninvited and not altogether welcome guest, was not to be denied. Sir Darrell insisted that he stay to sup with them before returning to Plymouth, and so Giles had yet another memory to carry away with him. Imelda in the soft glow of candlelight that flattered the creamy gold of her skin against the apricot gown, and struck burnished lights from the gleaming waves and curls of her brown hair. Mrs. Pennan was beautiful and Lady Conyngton most striking, but both might have been wrinkled hags for all the impression they made upon him. He saw only Imelda.

Charity, observing how his gaze lingered on the girl, and the expression in his eyes, was filled with dismay, for it told her that matters had gone past mending.

Imelda's feelings had been transparently clear to her from the first, and now it was plain that Giles Bradwell was as deeply in love with her as she with him—in spite of their correctly formal behaviour the fact was mirrored in their faces for all to see. Roxanne had noticed it, and had cast her ladyship a startled, questioning look, but Roxanne could be depended upon to sympathize with the young couple as greatly as did Charity herself.

Darrell was a different matter. Stealing a covert glance at him, his wife could tell, from his frown and the cold anger in his eyes, that he understood the situation only too well, and was not prepared to tolerate it. The obligation of a host to his guest must preclude any show of displeasure towards the Major, which meant that, inevitably, the full weight of that displeasure would fall presently upon Imelda. Charity's heart ached for her, for the glow of happiness so soon to be extinguished, but she knew that there was nothing she could do, except be ready to offer such comfort as she could when the time came.

Part 4

Imelda was busy at the spinning-wheel in the parlour, but her thoughts had nothing to do with the task in hand. That was the trouble with an occupation like spinning—when one was skilled at it through much practice it engaged the hands but not the mind, so that unhappiness could not be held at bay; and Imelda was desperately unhappy.

She could still recall every minute of the shattering interview she had had with Sir Darrell on the day after Giles's visit, more than two weeks ago. She had come to it all unsuspecting, still blissfully enfolded in the unspoken certainty that Giles cared for her, and innocently unaware that anyone else had discovered her secret, but that illusion was soon rudely dispelled. Darrell, confronted by her white face and stricken eyes, was not quite as severe as he had intended to be, but he left her in no doubt at all of his decision. She and Giles were never to meet again.

"I admit our debt to him, your own most of all," he told her, "but that obligation has no bearing at all upon the larger issue. Bradwell is opposed to everything we hold most sacred; everything for which your brothers fought and died. Gratitude alone cannot transform an enemy into a friend."

He added more in the same strain, and by the time he had done, Imelda felt like a traitress; to him and to Charity; to the King; to her father and the dead brothers she could scarcely remember. She wept, but it never occurred to her to defy Sir Darrell, for it had been impressed upon her before she left her home that henceforth he and his wife would stand to her in place of her own parents, and must be similarly obeyed.

Sir Darrell had left the Dower House two days later, bound for London—he had gone, though Imelda did not know this, in the forlorn hope of raising there the desperately needed loan he had failed to obtain in Exeter—and ever since she had been hoping against hope that Giles would come again before he returned. She would not be permitted to see him, but they had Lady Conyngton's sympathy, and surely, given an opportunity, her ladyship could make Giles understand? Imelda felt that she could only bear not seeing him again if she could be certain that he harboured no harsh thoughts of her.

Yet the days were going by and he had not come, and now she had begun to fear that even the opportunity for explanations would be lost. She looked at Charity, writing a letter at the small table by the window, and tried to find the courage to broach the subject, but before she could do so, a servant entered the room, bringing a note for her ladyship which he said had just been delivered by one of Mrs. Pennan's people. The interruption shattered the former atmosphere of comfortable intimacy which had seemed to invite confidences, and Imelda sighed and went on with her spinning.

A stifled sound drew her attention to her companion again, and her own troubles were immediately forgotten. Charity was sitting with Roxanne's note crushed in her hand; there was a stunned look on her face, and tears in her eyes. Imelda jumped up and rushed to her side.

"Cousin! Oh, what is it? What has happened?"

"Jonathan!" Charity said dazedly. "Little Jonathan Shenfield, Ellen's elder boy. He is dead."

"Dead?" Imelda repeated blankly. "But we saw him with his mother at church only two days ago, and he seemed in perfect health. Was there an accident?"

Charity shook her head. "He was taken ill during the night, Roxanne says, and died a few hours ago. She had just received the news, and delayed only to write this before going to the Moat House, but she promises to stop here on her way home to tell me more." She pressed her hands to her face. "Oh, poor Ellen! My aunt too—Jonathan meant so much to her! It must be like losing Jonas over again."

There was silence for a minute or two. Imelda stood with her arm about Charity's shoulders in unspoken sympathy, and thought of the sturdy, golden-haired little boy, bright-eyed and rosy-cheeked, walking beside his widowed mother along the path to the lych-gate. The death of a beloved child was an all too frequent tragedy, and yet it seemed incredible that so bonny a lad could have been so suddenly and fatally stricken. There was no sickness in the village; no plague or fever; what mysterious malady had ended that brief life?

"I helped to bring Jonathan into the world," Charity said unsteadily at length, "and was nurse to him and to his younger brother until my marriage." She sensed rather than saw Imelda's disbelieving stare, and added with a dreary, mirthless little smile: "You did not know, did you, that I was treated like a servant in my cousin's house?"

There seemed to be no answer to this. Imelda remained silent, trying to picture the assured Lady Conyngton, the gracious chatelaine of the Dower House, in a servant's place, and failing utterly. The Shenfields must always have been a strange, unhappy household.

"Jonathan was such a bonny child," Charity resumed after a moment. "He never ailed, even when he was a baby, yet now—!" She broke off, making a helpless gesture. "I cannot believe it!"

The news Roxanne had sent cast a shadow over them both, and Imelda was not surprised when Charity, abandoning her letter, went upstairs to the nursery. In any mother, she thought, the news of a child's death must prompt a fearful thanksgiving that her own little ones had been spared, and she would seek the reassurance of being with them and holding them in her arms. And yet—the rebellious thought came unbidden and would not be banished—Ellen Oliver, and little Mary, the daughter born six months after Jonas Shenfield's death; she still had her two younger babes, had had little Jonathan himself for six precious years. She had not been condemned to a lonely, barren existence in someone else's home, with only another woman's children to tend and love. While the spinning-wheel turned and thread grew beneath her skilful fingers, Imelda spun also a bitter-sweet daydream, of a house where she alone was mistress, and of a little son at her knee. The picture of the house was vague and shadowy, but the child she could see clearly; a tall, long-limbed little boy, with fair hair and serious, blue-grey eyes. . . .

She was roused from her reverie by the sound of hoof-beats, a swift thunder along the track from the road, a ringing clatter on the stones of the forecourt, and she sprang up from her stool with a sudden, sharp sense of foreboding. Running out into the hall, she was in time to see, through the open front door, Roxanne toss the reins to her groom and slide from the saddle without waiting for his assistance. Then, catching up her trailing skirts, she came stumbling up the few shallow steps to the door with equal haste. Her face was white and tense in its frame of auburn curls.

"Charity!" she said abruptly to Imelda. "Where is she?" and then, before the other girl could reply, was brushing past her, for Charity herself was coming quickly down the stairs.

"What is it, Roxanne? What news do you bring?"

"I have just come from the Moat House." Roxanne

was breathing hard, and there was anger and fear in her voice. "I think Mrs. Shenfield is mad. The shock of her grandson's death has turned her brain, for she declares that he was murdered—by witchcraft!"

Charity drew a sharp breath. "Is this Malperne's doing?"

Roxanne shook her head. "He is there, of course, but to do him justice he tried to calm her, and to check her wild accusations. Charity, I have not yet told you the worst!" She hesitated, looking at her friend with frightened troubled eyes. "Your aunt accuses *you* of being the witch who cast the fatal spell."

Roxanne's words seemed to echo still around the hall after she had finished speaking. Imelda choked back an exclamation of horror, while in the background, the serving-man who had come needlessly into the hall at the sound of Mrs. Pennan's arrival gaped unbelieving, but Charity herself, still standing on the lowest stair with her hand on the carved newel-post, was silent and statue-like, staring at Roxanne in utter stupefaction. It seemed to Imelda an incredibly long time before she spoke.

"She accuses *me*?"

"She was beside herself. She cannot seriously believe such a thing." Roxanne sounded as though she were trying to convince herself. "But I thought I should come at once to warn you. There were servants present. . . ."

The words trailed uneasily into silence, and she cast a desperate glance at Imelda, who looked helplessly back. Then Roxanne's words reminded her of the serving-man still staring in the doorway, and she said tentatively:

"Should we not go within?"

With an obvious effort Charity roused herself to agree, and came forward across the hall. Imelda stood aside to let her and Roxanne go past, and then followed them into the parlour and closed the door.

Charity went slowly to the day-bed which now stood by the window and sat down on it, still looking as though she could not believe what had happened. Imelda could scarcely believe it herself. Ellen Shenfield had foreseen danger, and so had Giles, but this was immeasurably worse than anything any of them had feared. Surely Roxanne was right, and shock and grief had turned Mrs. Shenfield's brain? Surely no one would believe that Charity could harm a child—any child—or be guilty of the abomination of witchcraft?

Even as she tried to reassure herself, she was aware of the cold stirring of fear. The witch-hunt was already up; it had claimed one life without waiting to learn whether or not its victim was guilty, and, in spite of Giles's stern warnings, might well claim another if Matty Weddon were found; and this was the horror which Elizabeth Shenfield's crazed accusations might well loose against her niece.

"*Why* does she accuse me?" Charity asked at length, and at once answered the question herself in a low voice. "Because she hates me, and hates Darrell, and has done so ever since Jonas died. But why does she believe that poor child died of witchcraft?"

"Because of the manner of his dying," Roxanne said reluctantly. "When their nurse put the children to bed he was well and happy, but during the night he woke screaming with pain, and nothing they could do brought him any relief. There were knives, he kept screaming, burning knives in his belly. Mrs. Shenfield sent to Plymouth for a physician, but before he could reach the Moat House the poor mite died, in dreadful agony."

Charity uttered a faint sound of horror and protest and bowed her face on her hands, and Imelda remembered that she had been nurse to the dead child for the first two years of his life. To Roxanne she said:

"Did the physician see him? Could he not tell what caused his death?"

Roxanne shook her head. "He was baffled, and ready enough to agree with Mrs. Shenfield that witchcraft was the cause." She hesitated, glancing at Charity. "It does seem very likely, for who now can doubt that there are witches in Conyngton? But to accuse Charity is monstrous."

Charity raised her head. She was dry-eyed, but very pale, and her voice was not quite steady as she asked: "What does Ellen believe?"

"That the witches murdered her child," Roxanne replied promptly, "but never that you had any hand in it. In fact, when Mrs. Shenfield first made the accusation, Ellen cried out against her with more spirit than I have ever known her to show towards her mother-in-law. She is heart-broken over Jonathan's death, but she will hear no word against you."

"God's blessing on her for that," Charity said softly. "Poor Ellen! Would that I might go to her, for we were close friends once." She looked at Roxanne. "Has word been sent to her father?"

"Be sure it has," Roxanne replied with some satisfaction. "*I* saw to that, even before I went to the Moat House, for I knew that if Mrs. Shenfield sent for anyone it would be Taynton. Ellen has a right to her own people about her in her time of sorrow."

"And Taynton?"

"By a merciful chance he is away from Plymouth at present on some matter of business. Malperne said so."

One enemy less to reckon with, Imelda thought thankfully, and yet Malperne and Mrs. Shenfield between them could be dangerous enough. What would happen if they complained to the authorities that Lady Conyngton practised witchcraft, and by it had caused the death of a child? One thing at least was certain; no Justice to whom such a complaint was made would dare to ignore it.

"Charity, should you not send word to Darrell?" Roxanne asked hesitantly, and Imelda realized that their thoughts had been following similar paths. "He would wish to be here to look after you if—if there are difficulties."

"Certainly not." Charity was recovering from the shock now, and her natural courage was reasserting itself. "The business which took him to London is far more important than any wild notions my aunt may take into her head. You said yourself that she is distraught with grief, and though *you* may be surprised that she shrieks out first at me, I assure you that I am not. She always disliked me, and since my marriage she hated me, and would like to blame me for every ill that befalls her. I have no doubt that when she is calmer she will realize the absurdity of such an accusation."

"*I* doubt it," Roxanne replied bluntly. "Distraught or calm, Mrs. Shenfield desires only to make mischief for you and Darrell, and he should be with you at such a time."

"That, my dear, is for me to decide," Charity reminded her gently. "You have allowed my aunt to frighten you, but she has never frightened me, and I do not intend that she shall do so now."

Roxanne started to argue, but was interrupted. A thunderous knocking sounded upon the front door, making them all jump, and after a minute or so the same servant who had witnessed Roxanne's arrival came into the room. He looked both angry and alarmed.

"Dr. Malperne be here, m'lady, demanding to see you."

Imelda felt her heart give a sickening lurch of fright, and guessed that both her companions felt the same. It was a moment or two before Charity spoke.

"Is he alone?"

"Aye, m'lady."

"Then admit him."

Reluctantly the man turned and threw wide the door, and the preacher stalked into the room, looking, thought Imelda, more than ever like some dark bird of ill-omen. His face was haggard with sleeplessness and black-stubbled about mouth and chin, for he had been summoned hurriedly to the Moat House in the middle of the night, but his sombre, deep-sunken eyes burned with undiminished fire. He halted in the middle of the room, looking from one young woman to the other, and then addressed Charity in his deep, harsh voice.

"I came to tell your ladyship that your small kinsman, Jonathan Shenfield, is dead of witchcraft, and yourself accused by your good aunt of causing his death, but I see that Mrs. Pennan is before me."

Charity had risen to her feet to confront him. She was as tall as he, and looked levelly back at him, pale but quite composed.

"And you, sir? Do *you* accuse me?"

"Not yet, my lady," he replied unexpectedly. "It is not to be denied that foul witchcraft killed the child, but the powers of Hell which are now let loose upon this miserable parish may well deceive even the godly with their subtleties of evil, and we must be sure that none are accused without due cause. I have urged Mrs. Shenfield to pray that the Lord grant her grace to see clearly whether such cause to accuse you truly exists. Her natural grief over the loss of a loved grandchild may have made her vulnerable to the voice of the Prince of Lies."

"The child's mother sees no such cause," Roxanne reminded him boldly. "She rejects such accusations out of hand."

"I have not forgotten it, madam," Malperne replied, "nor do I forget that as a babe, the boy was for two years in her ladyship's care, and came to no harm." He looked again towards Charity, demanding sternly: "Madam, I charge you to tell me truly, is there any recent quarrel between your aunt and you?"

Charity sighed. "Dr. Malperne, you know as well as I do that the quarrel is all upon one side. We would live at peace with her, but she will not have it so. No more stands between us now than at the time of my marriage. I grieve for little Jonathan, and for his mother and grandmother, and I swear to you before God that I had no hand in his death."

"Swear not," he rebuked her sternly. "I must think on this matter, and pray that my duty be made plain to me. At present Mrs. Shenfield is your only accuser, nor is there evidence to support the charge against you, but I warn you, my lady, that if any just cause be found, I shall myself accuse you before the law. It matters not to me whether a witch be of high degree or low."

Without waiting for a reply he swung round and strode from the room, and they heard his footsteps receding across the hall. Charity sat down again, rather abruptly, on the day-bed, and Imelda, after one searching glance at her, went quickly to the cupboard to fetch her a glass of wine.

"He's afraid," Roxanne said shrewdly. "He had a sharp fright in Plymouth after old Tabitha was killed, and dreads what may befall him if he raises another witch-hunt. That is why he tried to prevent Mrs. Shenfield from accusing you."

"No." Charity spoke unsteadily but with absolute conviction. "He is not afraid. Cautious, perhaps, and resolved this time to act strictly within the law, but if he comes to believe me guilty he will accuse me as fearlessly as he would denounce the humblest beggar-woman. That I know."

There followed seemingly endless days of mounting tension. Within hours, Mrs. Shenfield's accusations against her niece had become common knowledge, and though the people of Conyngton remained solidly united in loyalty to their squire and in a refusal to believe ill of his wife, the old neighbourliness had vanished. It might be unthinkable that her ladyship would practice witchcraft, but that it was being practised in the parish no one could any longer doubt, and every inhabitant was suspicious of his fellows. Fear and distrust spread like some virulent contagion; there were no longer meetings of friendly gossip on the green, or convival gatherings of the Conyngton Arms; even the children no longer laughed and played together, while the smallest dispute with a neighbour was followed by hours and days of anxiety lest the disagreement had aroused the spite of one of the followers of Satan.

On the Sabbath Dr. Malperne again preached savagely against the evil of witchcraft, but added a stern admonition that, while all should be watchful to detect the guilty, no accusation must be made without due cause, or otherwise than to the Justices. This far, at least, his experience in Plymouth had curbed his fanaticism.

Not even this warning, however, prevented an ugly incident by the lych-gate. According to custom Charity, accompanied by Imelda and Roxanne, was first to leave the church, followed by Mrs. Shenfield and Ellen, who were escorted on this occasion by Ellen's father. Little Oliver was clinging to his mother's hand,

and it was inevitable that the thoughts of everyone present should turn to the other little boy who, only a week before, had walked beside her, but who yesterday had been laid in the family tomb beside his father and grandfather. Ellen was weeping softly as she leaned on her father's arm, and Charity, though well aware of the unwisdom of it, felt that she could not let her pass without a word of sympathy and comfort.

She stepped forward, saying gently, "Ellen, my dear," but the words were cut short as Mrs. Shenfield, moving with a swiftness startling in one of her girth, snatched Oliver up in her arms and whirled him away as though from the vicinity of some venomous serpent, thrusting him into her coach and setting herself protectively before it, right fist out-thrust with the first and fourth finger extended in the ancient gesture of defence against the powers of darkness.

She could not more definitely or publicly have stated her belief in her niece's guilt. Charity went white, and a little murmur arose among the people streaming out of church—a murmur of dismay from the villagers and of angry satisfaction from the Moat House servants. Ellen gave a sob and buried her face against her father's shoulder, and over her bowed head he looked helplessly at Charity and then at Roxanne. From somewhere at the back of the crowd a clod of dried earth came flying past him to strike the ground at Charity's feet and spatter her skirts with dust, and he said urgently in a low voice:

"My lady, get you home—and keep your servants close about you."

Dazedly she accepted the advice and turned away

to where the black mare was tethered, and as the two girls followed her, Mr. Pennan added protestingly:

"Roxanne!"

His daughter-in-law paused and looked back; then she shook her head. "No, sir," she said quietly, "I know what Tom would wish me to do," and she followed Charity towards the horses.

In silence, more disturbed by the incident than any of them was willing to admit, they rode up the hill, and Imelda, for one, was thankful when the familiar surroundings of the Dower House were once more about them. There was a sense of safety there, and though she knew this to be illusory, it was none the less comforting.

Early on Tuesday morning, so early that the household was only just dispersing after morning prayers, there was again a flurry of hoof-beats before the Dower House, and again Roxanne came hastening anxiously up the steps and into the hall, but this time she was not alone. This time her father-in-law came with her.

They were met by Charity, still holding the Bible from which she had been reading to her assembled household, for in Darrell's absence she conducted the prayers herself. Imelda was with her, while one or two of the upper servants, hearing the visitor's arrival, lingered uneasily to learn the reason for it. Charity looked from Roxanne's white face to Mr. Pennan's grave countenance, and instinctively braced herself to bear whatever fresh blow they were about to deal her.

"Charity, we must speak with you," Roxanne announced without preamble. "Privately."

"Of course." Charity's voice was steady, and her manner had lost none of its gracious dignity. "Come within."

She led the way to the parlour, beckoning to Imelda to follow, and while Mr. Pennan closed the door behind them, she handed the Bible to the girl.

"Put that away for me, my dear, if you please," she said quietly. "Well, Roxanne?"

"It is your aunt Elizabeth," Roxanne said in a low voice. "She lies close to death, stricken"—she hesitated—"by witchcraft."

Imelda, laying the family Bible in the carved, silver-bound casket where it lived, spun round to stare, horrified, at the speaker. Charity put out her hand rather quickly and gripped the back of a chair; it was a moment or two before she spoke.

"Are you sure?"

"Certain, my lady." It was Mr. Pennan who replied, his voice, like his lean, kindly face, grave and troubled. "Last night, when Mrs. Shenfield's woman turned back the cover so that her mistress might climb into bed, there beneath them was a small image of baked clay, fashioned in your aunt's likeness and clad in black weeds and veil. There were two long pins driven through its breast."

He went on to describe how Mrs. Shenfield, on seeing the image, had uttered a shriek which rang through the house and sent Ellen, her father and sundry servants hastening to her room, where they found her lying in a swoon and her waiting-woman almost out of her wits with terror. Between them they had managed to get Mrs. Shenfield into bed—from which

Mr. Pennan himself had removed the horrible little effigy—and restored her to consciousness, but nothing could convince her that sentence of death had not been passed upon her. Even Dr. Malperne, whom Daniel Stotewood had hastened to summon from the village, had been unable to reassure her, though he spent the night in prayer at her bedside.

"So at first light he borrowed a fleet horse from the stables and set out for Plymouth," Mr. Pennan concluded, and added significantly: "Taking that accursed image with him."

A little silence fell, for they all knew, without any need to put it into words, what the preacher had gone to do; and against whom the charge of witchcraft would be levelled. Mrs. Shenfield had been Charity's only accuser; she had made public declaration of her belief; and now the powers of evil had been invoked against her, with terrible effect.

"Charity, what will you do?" Roxanne asked at length in a frightened voice. "As soon as Mr. Pennan came to tell me what had happened, I knew we must warn you, but—!" She hesitated, and then repeated helplessly: "What will you do?"

Charity spoke through stiff lips. "What can I do, except wait, and pray? I am innocent of these foul crimes, and I must have faith that truth and justice will prevail." She turned to Mr. Pennan. "Sir, I am more grateful to you than I can say for coming here, and I dare to hope it means that you, at least, have not condemned me out of hand."

The shrewd blue eyes regarded her gravely, but not unkindly. "My lady, foul witchcraft is at work here," he said bluntly. "It has murdered my innocent grand-son, and I am told that, beside your aunt, one of the villagers lies stricken of it. That cannot be denied. As to who is guilty of this abomination, that is for those wiser than I to discover, though it occurs to me to wonder why, if your ladyship is indeed possessed of evil powers, you did not invoke them long ago, when you suffered under your kinsman's tyranny." He turned to Roxanne. "I must go back to the Moat House, for Ellen will need me. Do you come with me, daughter?"

"I will come directly, sir. Tell Ellen so."

"Perhaps you should go now, Roxanne," Charity suggested gently. "I dare not hope that all will treat me as generously as Mr. Pennan has done, and for the present my company will be better avoided."

"Yes, indeed," Roxanne agreed cordially, "and no doubt Imelda should come with me, so that she is not endangered either. My dear friend, do you suppose that either of us would desert you now?"

"Or ever?" Imelda added, and came impulsively to catch Charity's hand in both of hers. "But, cousin, our support alone cannot give you the comfort you need. Will you not send for Sir Darrell?"

"Your kinswoman gives good advice, my lady," Mr. Pennan agreed emphatically. "If you know where your husband may be reached, I counsel you most strongly to send word to him without delay."

Charity thank him, and later, when Roxanne had followed her father-in-law to the Moat House, she did write a letter to Darrell, but, Imelda noted with dis-quiet, made no attempt to despatch it. She did not dare to interfere, but could not help feeling that, no matter how vital the business which had taken the squire to London, it should not be allowed to take precedence over the danger which now threatened his wife.

That the danger was very real, no one at the Dower House doubted. The servants there would remain loyal to their mistress whatever befell, but by Wednesday morning the bailiff, having been to the village, confided to Imelda that though Dr. Malperne had not yet returned he had seen several strangers there, townsmen, from Plymouth, of the most fanatical kind. They were haranguing the villagers on the evil of witches in general and Lady Conyngton in particular, and though most of the people scorned the suggestion that her ladyship was the author of their present ills, one or two waverers were beginning to question, while servants from the Moat House, those "foreigners" who usually held aloof, were going boldly about trying to stir up feeling against her.

Charity herself, outwardly composed, was yet conscious of a cold weight of fear which was with her through every waking moment and invaded her fitful slumbers with hideous nightmares, but in spite of the horrible threat hanging over her, she was still mistress of a household, and found a certain measure of comfort in keeping to the familiar pattern of daily tasks. It was a pattern soon to be rudely shattered.

Charity was in the stillroom with Rebecca that Wednesday noontide when the door was thrown open and Imelda appeared, her face as white as the broad collar of her lavender-coloured gown. Charity looked at her, sudden foreboding making it impossible for her to speak.

"Cousin," Imelda said breathlessly, "Major Bradwell is here! I saw him from the window as he rode out from the wood."

Charity felt a surge of relief that was almost anger. So that was why the silly child looked so stricken, because Giles Bradwell had come, and she was forbidden to see him. She drew a deep breath, and spoke more sharply than she had ever done to the girl.

"Then you will remain here with Rebecca, and finish the task upon which she and I were engaged. I will make your apologies to the Major, and explain to him why we can no longer receive him."

Imelda shook her head; her eyes were tragic. "You do not understand! He does not come now as a guest. There are a dozen or more soldiers with him."

Giles dismounted, and stood for a moment looking up at the gracious frontage of the Dower House. Behind him, the forecourt was full of the clatter and jingle and glitter of his little troop; before him, at the top of the shallow steps, the great oak door stood open to the shadowy coolness of the panelled hall, with its great stone fireplace on one side, and the broad stairway rising in short, right-angled flights on the other. There was the scent of flowers from the garden, and of freshly scythed grass from the orchard beyond.

He hated the duty he had come to do, even though he had used every means he could think of to be assigned to it. Someone must do it, and better he than a stranger, one of the fanatical sectaries with which the New Model was beset, but though he knew that, he knew, too, what the doing of it might cost him; but a soldier must not count the cost to himself. . . . He squared his shoulders, and resolutely mounted the steps.

Charity Conyngton was coming slowly down the stairs. Imelda was with her, while at the head of the staircase the maidservant with the scarred features stood leaning her hands on the balustrade and staring down. Giles took one look at Imelda, saw the fear and the reproach in her white face, and thereafter kept his gaze fixed firmly upon her ladyship.

Imelda herself was there with no thought of defying Sir Darrell's commands—it was for Charity's sake alone. In that heart-stopping moment when an idle glance from a window had shown her Giles leading his soldiers towards the house, and she realized the purpose for which he must have come, she had realized, too, the truth of everything Darrell had said to her. No Cromwellian was, or ever could be, anything but an enemy to those of their blood. She had toyed with the idea of appealing to Giles for help, yet here he was, with all the trappings of a hated tyranny, to do the very thing against which she would have sought his protection.

They reached the foot of the stairs, and paused. Giles was coming across the hall towards them, a hand on the hilt of his sword, his face in the helmet's shadow the face of a stranger. He halted a couple of yards away and stood looking grimly at Charity.

"My Lady Conyngton"—the deep voice was curt and authoritative, wholly unemotional; they could not know with what an effort he kept it so—"I am here to escort you to Plymouth, where your presence is required to answer certain charges made against you. You stand accused of witchcraft, and of murder by the powers of witchcraft."

Charity's expression did not change, and only he, and Imelda standing close beside her, were aware of the little quiver of shock that ran through her. After a moment, when she was sure she could command her voice, she asked quietly:

"Who accuses me?"

"Dr. Malperne, your preacher, and Mr. Edward Taynton, a citizen of Plymouth," he replied formally, and added with no change of tone: "Pray desire your servants to pack such necessities as you will require, and to saddle a horse for you. Meanwhile you will wait in this room."

He crossed the hall and threw open the door of the parlour. Charity looked at the servants who had come pressing through the doorway leading to the domestic quarters, singled out the most senior of them and said in the same quiet voice:

"See that Major Bradwell's orders are carried out. Hereafter you will obey Miss Hallett as you would myself, until Sir Darrell returns."

For a few seconds no one made any move to carry out her orders. There was a mutter of anger and defiance, and Giles said warningly, in the same curt tone as before:

"Resistance will harm rather than help your mistress. I have force enough with me to curb any you may offer, so do not put me to the necessity of using it."

Still they hesitated, until Charity spoke again. She was still outwardly calm, but Imelda could see with what grim determination she was clinging to her self-possession.

"There will be no hindrance of my departure. I know your loyalty, and need no proof of it save that my present commands be obeyed. See to it, I pray you."

She turned and went quickly across the hall and past Giles into the parlour. Imelda followed, daring him with one furious glance to forbid her, and saw with concern that once out of sight of the servants, Charity's self-command had failed her. She had dropped into a chair by the table and was sitting with her face buried in her hands. Imelda, hurrying to cast comforting arms about her, turned on Giles with a fury of which her grief and terror for Charity were only a part.

"So this is how a Roundhead repays hospitality! The guest of yesterday becomes an enemy leading soldiers against a defenceless woman," she accused him, and added contemptuously: "Judas!"

"Imelda!" Charity raised her head; her voice shook. "You are unjust. I believe I have cause to be grateful to Major Bradwell."

"Grateful?" Imelda repeated bitterly. "For this?"

"For the courtesy he is using towards me. Do you imagine such treatment is commonly accorded a woman accused as I am accused?"

Imelda was silenced. She had seen the flash of pain in Giles's eyes as she berated him, the paling of his tanned cheeks and the betraying quiver of a muscle beside his mouth, and for one brief instant had rejoiced in wounding him. Now she was ashamed. She remembered Tabitha, the broken, bleeding victim of the mob, and how Giles would have protected even her had he arrived in time. Since this terrible thing had befallen Charity, how much better for her to be Giles's prisoner than any other's.

He was addressing Charity as though Imelda had not spoken. "My lady, I know your husband is away from home. If you will accept advice from me, I counsel you to send him word of your plight if you can, and that as speedily as may be."

"Yes." Charity pressed a hand to her head. "I wrote a letter yesterday, when I heard what had happened, to my aunt. Imelda, you must send it. Add one of your own, telling him what has now befallen me. His direction is on my letter."

Her voice was trembling too much for her to continue, and she was obliged to pause to try to regain control over it. Giles said gently—and Imelda wondered with a stab of anguish if she would ever again hear the deep voice address *her* in that tone:

"Have you a trustworthy messenger to send?"

"Yes." Charity drew a deep breath and looked at Imelda. "Barnaby must go. He followed Sir Darrell to the wars, and is resourceful and loyal. Tell him to make inquiries along the road, for it may be that Sir Darrell has already set out for home. He will need money for the journey." With shaking fingers, she unfastened the bunch of keys that swung from her waist by a silver chain, and held them out. "Take these. You will need them, for that and for other matters."

Imelda took the keys reluctantly, for there was a finality about the gesture which struck her with a sense of foreboding. Defying it, she said:

"I will guard them carefully, cousin, until you return. Trust me."

"I do, my dear, and give thanks that you are here." The ghost of a smile flickered about Charity's lips for a second, and was gone. "Major Bradwell, I have one favour to ask you. May I say goodbye to my children?"

"Of course, my lady," he replied promptly, but then hesitated. "It will be necessary, I fear, for one of my men to go with you, but do not be alarmed. I chose carefully those who ride with me today, and you will find no bigots among them."

She nodded, and rose to her feet. Giles opened the door and called for his sergeant, who, when he came, proved to be a reassuringly cheery-looking man with a weather-beaten face and kindly eyes. He seemed to find nothing untoward in his commander's bearing towards an accused witch, and regarded Charity with nothing more than curiosity.

"Sergeant, I have given Lady Conyngton permission to take leave of her children. Go with her to the nursery and stay within hearing, but keep out of sight. No need to frighten the little ones."

The sergeant saluted and stepped aside for Charity to precede him, falling in close behind her as she crossed the hall to the stairs. Giles closed the door again, and turned. Imelda, still standing by Charity's chair and fidgeting with the keys she held, said hurriedly, without looking at him:

"Forgive me. What I said was unjust, and I had no right—!"

"It is no matter. You are naturally concerned for Lady Conyngton." He brushed the attempted apology curtly aside as though it were of no importance, and passed on to more urgent matters. "Write that letter to Conyngton as soon as we have gone, and send the man off with it at once. Give him this for the journey."

He had come towards her as he spoke, and she saw that he was holding out a weighty purse. In the blankest astonishment her gaze flew upward to his face.

"I cannot take that! Sir Darrell would never permit—!"

"No one need know of it save you and I. Her ladyship has given you her household keys." She still hesitated, and he added impatiently: "Come, take it! This is no time for empty pride. A full purse can command the fleetest horses. Do you not yet realize the urgency of this affair?"

She allowed him to thrust the purse into her hand; was scarcely aware of taking it as her frightened gaze searched his face, seeking reassurance.

"Surely they can never prove so absurd a charge against her?"

"Taynton and Malperne will do their best, and no one can tell what the outcome will be. I know that neither the civil nor the military authorities were eager to have her made prisoner, for Conyngton still wields wide influence in the countryside and to charge his wife with witchcraft is a very different matter from charging some friendless old crone. For the present they will proceed with caution, which is why I was able to secure the task of coming here today, and why I believe that even in Plymouth she will be treated with the consideration due to her rank. Much will depend upon the weight of evidence brought against her."

"There *is* no real evidence. Only the accusations of Malperne and Mrs. Shenfield, and this man Taynton. All enemies of the Conyngtons."

He knew that often accusation alone was sufficient to ensure conviction on a charge of witchcraft, but he would not add to Imelda's burden of worry by telling her so. Neither would he lie to her, buoying her up with empty reassurances that all would be well, so, to avoid the necessity of doing neither, he continued briskly:

"Her ladyship should carry with her such money as can be spared. I am sure that she will be tolerably well treated, but any imprisonment can be made easier if the means are at hand to purchase additional comforts. You had better see to that—and hide that purse, if no one else is to know of it."

"Yes." Imelda spoke uncertainly, reminding herself that it was Charity's danger that mattered, and not whether Giles would ever forgive the insult she had flung at him. The curtness of his voice, and his formal manner, seemed to hold out scant hope of pardon, but she thrust her own personal wretchedness aside and hurried away to do his bidding. He seemed intent upon doing everything in his power to help Charity, and that was the most important thing.

When she had gone, Giles stood for a while deep in thought, frowning, and drumming his fingers on the dark, polished wood of the table beside him. He was totally convinced of Lady Conyngton's innocence of the charges against her, but he was under no illusion regarding her danger. The predominantly Royalist west of England was not like the north and the east, with their extreme Puritan or Presbyterian beliefs and their vivid memories of the great witch-hunts of the previous decade, but witchcraft was rightly feared and hated by all Christians no matter what creed they followed; and witchcraft was undoubtedly rampant in Conyngton St. John. Rumours of the child's death and his grandmother's suspicions had reached Plymouth well in advance of Dr. Malperne's formal accusation, and Giles, fearing danger to Imelda as well as to Charity, had done the only thing he could think of which might help to avert that danger, but he had no means of knowing whether the aid he had asked for would come in time. Or even if it would come at all. . . .

Imelda's reaction to his errand today had been much as he had feared it would be, but that did not prevent him from resenting it. "Judas!" The bitter insult rankled still; in the circumstances he could have forgiven a great deal, but—perhaps because of his own uncomfortable feeling of treachery—he found it impossible to forgive that.

He was glad that Imelda did not come back to the parlour before the sergeant returned to report that all was in readiness for their departure, and though she was in the hall when he went out, it was at his prisoner that he looked, and not at her. Charity was very pale, and he thought she had been weeping, but she looked quite composed and he felt a surge of admiration for her courage, guessing how hard won that composure must be.

When she saw him come out of the parlour, Charity turned to Imelda. "I leave all in your charge, my dear," she said quietly, "knowing that I may do so with an easy mind. Comfort the children as best you can. I have tried to make them understand that I must go away for a time, but they are so little—!" Her voice broke, and she leaned quickly forward to kiss the girl on the cheek.

"Cousin!" Imelda flung her arms round her and for a moment they clung tightly together. Then Charity, as though afraid that her precarious self-control would break, put Imelda aside, made a blind gesture of farewell towards the watching, weeping servants and went quickly to the door where Giles stood waiting for her.

At a sign from him, the sergeant escorted her down the steps to where one of her own servants held the bridle of the black mare, and another waited to lift her into the saddle. Giles looked once at Imelda, where she stood with the back of her hand pressed to her lips to hold back the tears; their eyes met for one bitter moment and then he turned sharp on his heel and followed his prisoner down the steps. A moment's pause, a sharp command, and then with a clatter of hooves and jingle of accoutrements they were gone, the noise of their going fading with a sound of finality on the warm, sunlit air.

Part 5

For what seemed a very long time after Charity and her escort had passed out of sight, Imelda stood without moving, while the tears which there was no longer any need to check ran unheeded down her cheeks. A sense of desolation possessed her; she wept for Charity and for Darrell; for the frightened, bewildered children in the nursery, for herself and for Giles, and for the gulf of anger and misunderstanding which had suddenly opened between them, making a mockery of all that had gone before. It seemed as though they had all been caught up by the insidious force of evil which had so stealthily taken possession of Conyngton St. John, and which now, the need for secrecy passing as its power grew, was spreading its dark and sinister shadow over them all. They were as much the victims of the witches as Elizabeth Shenfield, lying doomed and hopeless at the Moat House.

At last awareness of the need for action forced itself through her wretchedness. She turned to send away the whispering, anxious servants, and realized with a start of dismay that Rebecca Moone was standing beside her, looking, as Imelda herself had done, in the direction taken by the soldiers. The unmarked side of the woman's face was towards her, and Imelda was startled by the expression of controlled fury in it. The other servants might weep; Rebecca looked as though she were calling down a curse on the departing troop.

"The soldiers are but the instrument of law, Rebecca," Imelda reminded her, and wondered even as she spoke what prompted her to say it. "Lady Conyngton's real enemies are those who make false accusation against her."

"I know it, madam," Rebecca spoke without turning, and the same smouldering anger sounded in her voice, "but did the red-coat Major not have a kindness for you, you would have seen with what savage zeal these Ironside soldiers commonly perform an errand such as this. Fortunate for this household that *he* led them. They did not even make a search."

"A search?" Imelda was bewildered. "For what?"

"For evidence of witchcraft. I looked to see them ransack the house from attic to cellar."

"They would have found nothing, for such evidence does not exist. Perhaps it would have been better if they *had* searched."

"Would it?" There was a sneering note now in

Rebecca's voice. "It's plain you know no more of the Ironsides than you have learned from your tall young Major, and he, I'll warrant, has used you gently enough. Best pray that's all you ever know."

She turned abruptly away without waiting for a reply, and walked across the hall and up the stairs, leaving Imelda in a turmoil of anger, humiliation and pain. It was obvious that, with Charity gone, Rebecca had no intention of according her deputy any respect at all, but though Imelda was uneasily aware that some of the other servants had heard the woman's insolent innuendo, she was relieved to find that they obeyed her without question when she told them to return to their work. Singling out the man Barnaby, she instructed him to make ready for a journey, and presently, having written the most difficult letter of her life, dispatched him on his unhappy errand.

News of Charity's arrest soon reached Roxanne, and she came at once to the Dower House, but in spite of the company—and she spent as much time there as she possibly could—the next three days were the longest and loneliest Imelda had ever spent. Mr. Pennan had returned to Plymouth as soon as he learned that Edward Taynton was one of Charity's accusers, but no word came from him, or from Giles.

In the village, so the bailiff reported, matters were going from bad to worse. Weddon the smith still suffered his death-in-life, dependent upon others for his every need; his two sons now openly declared their belief in Lady Conyngton's guilt, and others were beginning to agree with them. More frightening still, thanks to the zealots from Plymouth, she now seemed to figure as leader of the witches.

"But of 'em all, the worst be Daniel Stotewood," the bailiff informed Imelda darkly. "Peter Bramble told me as him and those with him even raised an outcry against her ladyship when the soldiers took her through the village t'other day, and might have done worse save that Major Bradwell made his men draw close all about her, and himself threatened Stotewood and his crew that if they didn't stand aside he'd ride 'em down."

Imelda shivered, realizing for the first time why Giles had led so large a party that day. At the time it had seemed to her just a gratuitous insult, a dozen of Cromwell's Ironsides to secure one woman; now she knew that his purpose had been simply to protect his prisoner, and she felt a fresh pang of remorse for her behaviour towards him.

That was on Friday morning, and it was not until the following day, when the shadows were already lengthening towards evening, that the first news from Plymouth reached them. Roxanne was at the Dower House and she and Imelda were in the nursery, in anxious consultation with Nurse, for the baby, Anne, had been fretful and troublesome all day, when a serving-maid opened the door and nervously announced that Major Bradwell was below.

Imelda's heart gave such a leap of mingled hope and dread that for a moment she could not speak. Roxanne managed to ask, in a voice unlike her own:

"Is he alone?"

"Aye, madam." The girl's frightened glance passed to Imelda. "He asked for Miss Hallett."

"He must have brought news of her ladyship," Roxanne said in the same odd voice. "God send it be good!" She half turned to the door, then checked, and cast a perceptive glance at her friend. "Go down, Imelda. I will come directly, when Nurse and I have decided what best to do for the child."

Imelda nodded wordlessly and went out. The nursery was on the second floor of the house, and she walked down the first steep and twisting stair, and then the broad, handsome flight to the hall, without being aware of doing so. She was longing to see Giles again, yet afraid to face him after the manner of their parting; impatient for the news he must have brought, yet fretful what it might be. Three days of gnawing anxiety, and three endless, sleepless nights, had brought her close to breaking-point, and yet she knew she must not break, not while the whole responsibility of the children and the household rested upon her.

The parlour door had been left ajar, and swung silently open when she touched it. Giles was standing by the window looking out into the garden where flowers hung drooping in the breathless summer heat; he was bareheaded, for the heavy steel helmet rested with his riding gauntlets on the table, and as Imelda stepped into the room he lifted an impatient hand to push the thick fair hair back from his forehead. Somehow the almost boyish gesture, and the sheer relief of seeing him, big and competent and infinitely reassuring, brought a sudden start of tears to her eyes. She pushed the door gently shut behind her, and the click of the latch brought him swinging round.

She saw the look of uncertainty in his face change immediately to loving concern. He stepped quickly forward with outstretched hands, and then without intending it, or even knowing exactly how it had happened, she was in his arms and it was as though their differences had never been. Their embrace was long and almost desperate, but when at length they drew a little apart to look into each other's eyes, she said in a fluttering whisper:

"No! We should not—!"

"No," he agreed seriously, "this is not the time, but now it must be said. I love you, Imelda. I have loved you since that first day, when we journeyed here together."

"I, too," she confessed shyly. "When you said farewell to me then, and I thought we should never meet again, I did not know how I was to bear it, but oh, Giles! Before Sir Darrell went away he forbade me ever to see you again."

"Believe me," he replied gently, "I know all the obstacles which stand between us, but if you will give me leave to hope, I will not admit defeat until I have striven against each and every one of them. Only you must think well what it would mean, my dear one. To marry me, you may have to sever all ties with your own family, with their beliefs and loyalties, and with their way of life." He saw that she was about to speak, and laid his hand lightly across her mouth. "No, do not answer me yet. The time is not yet come when we may turn our minds wholly to our own concerns."

He took her face between his hands and kissed her again, very tenderly this time, and though she heeded him enough not to reply in words, the response of her lips to his was answer enough; a wordless surrender, and an unspoken promise. For a few moments longer they clung together, and then, as the meaning of his latter words penetrated her mind, she drew back, looking up at him with conscience-stricken eyes.

"Charity!" she exclaimed contritely. "Oh, how could I have forgotten! Giles, how fares she?"

The pause before he replied was infinitesimal but she was aware of it, and it struck her with a cold fear which not even the reassurance of his next words could dispel.

"Well enough, I give you my word. She is imprisoned, of course, but in a decent room and with a tolerable degree of comfort. I had that from one who has seen her place of confinement, so you must not be picturing her in a dungeon."

"She has not been brought to trial?"

"No, and it is not yet certain that she will be. The Justices have questioned her, but at present they seek only to determine whether there is sufficient evidence to bring a charge of witchcraft against her. As I told you before, they proceed cautiously, for this is a delicate matter."

"And the evidence still rests solely upon the accusations of Mr. Taynton and Dr. Malperne?"

Again that tiny pause. "Yes, and they have both been questioned also. Moreover, it is to her ladyship's advantage that a search has revealed no witch-mark upon her body." He saw horror leap into Imelda's eyes, and added quickly: "No, love, not as that poor crone in the village was searched. This was done privately, with her ladyship's consent, and only certain well-respected matrons were present."

The hideous vision of a public ordeal similar to Tabitha's receded, but Imelda was not completely comforted, for she could appreciate, as a man could not, the humiliation Charity must have suffered through such a search, no matter how discreetly it was conducted. Before she could question him further, however, they heard light, hurried footsteps crossing the hall, and Roxanne came into the parlour.

She wasted no time in civilities apart from the briefest acknowledgement of Giles's greeting, but immediately demanded what news he brought. Imelda watched him while he repeated what he had already told her, and the certainty that he was keeping something back grew steadily stronger.

"There is something else," she said with conviction when he paused. "Something you are reluctant to tell us." He looked at her, frowning a little, and she laid her hand on his arm looking up into his face. "Giles, I can see it in your eyes. In the name of pity, tell me what it is."

Roxanne's brows lifted a fraction, but she made no comment. Giles said unwillingly:

"Yes, there is something else. Taynton has made further accusations against Lady Conyngton, accusations which reach back several years."

They stared at him, both guessing at least a part of what he was about to tell them. Roxanne put it into words.

"The death of her cousin, Jonas Shenfield?"

Giles nodded. "That is one charge. Since it has never been explained *why* Shenfield went to the ruined manor that night, Taynton accuses her ladyship of luring him there by unholy arts, and by the same means bringing about his death. He argues that Shenfield would have known the danger he courted by entering the ruins in the teeth of a gale, and so would never have gone there of his own free will. Also that it cannot be denied Shenfield's death made possible his kinswoman's marriage to Sir Darrell."

The two girls looked at each other in dismay. This was dangerous indeed, suggesting as it did that if Charity were an adept of the black-arts her witchhood was no recent thing, and accusing her of causing an event which had undoubtedly given her her dearest desire. Then Imelda remembered something else.

"You said 'that is one charge.' You cannot mean that there are more?"

"There is one more," he admitted reluctantly. "Taynton swears that four years ago, before her marriage, Lady Conyngton used enchantments to make his wife, her cousin Sarah, betray him."

Roxanne smote her hands angrily together. "Of what next will he accuse her? *I* can tell you the truth of that matter. Jonas Shenfield forced his young sister to marry Taynton, whom she detested and who used her so ill that within two years she fled from his house, and eloped with the man whom she had always loved. Charity aided their flight and Taynton has never forgiven her for it, but he must be crazed if he thinks to prove that she had to use witchcraft to bring about their elopement. The whole parish knows how unwillingly Sarah Shenfield went to her marriage."

"Perhaps so," Giles said slowly, "but this at least explains why Taynton is so bitter against her ladyship. No man could forget such dishonour."

"To my mind," Roxanne informed him tartly, "Taynton's dishonour lay in forcing wedlock upon so unwilling a maid. Nor is it lessened by his venting his vindictiveness upon Charity, just because his wife and her lover are beyond his reach."

"It does him scant credit, I confess," Giles admitted thoughtfully. "Tell me, Mrs. Pennan, are these facts widely known?"

"It happened before I came to Conyngton, but I would suppose that the whole neighbourhood rang with the tale, for Sarah Taynton eloped on the day before her brother met his death," Roxanne replied frankly. "Why do you ask?"

"Because it occurs to me that if it can be shown that this charge is unfounded, and prompted by malice, Taynton's other accusations against her ladyship may carry less weight. It is already common knowledge that Mrs. Shenfield bears a grudge against her niece." He paused, frowning. "What news of the lady?"

Roxanne sighed. "The same. She has not left her bed since the image was found, will scarcely touch food and complains ever of pain in her breast. Knowing herself doomed, she now waits fearfully for death to claim her."

"As it will," Giles said grimly, "unless the true source of this abomination can soon be traced."

He hesitated, for he had not intended to say anything of his own measures to achieve this, for fear of raising hopes which might not be fulfilled, but his resolve was not proof against the wariness and anxiety in Imelda's pale face. He could not, as he yearned to do, shoulder the whole of her burden of care, but he might be able to lighten it a little.

"We three," he continued abruptly, "and some few others have not the smallest doubt of Lady Conyngton's innocence, but even we cannot deny that witches *are* about their hellish work in Conyngton St. John, and the only way to save her ladyship is to discover them and bring them to justice. The authorities in Plymouth will not do this. If they decided there is enough evidence against her ladyship to bring her to trial, they will look to her to name her accomplices."

Imelda shuddered. The laws of England, unlike those of other lands, forbade the use of torture to discover witches, but there were still many painful and humiliating ordeals to which a suspect might legally be subjected in the hope of extracting information.

"How, then?" she asked wretchedly. "Are we to go searching for them ourselves?"

"The Lord forbid!" he exclaimed involuntarily, appalled by the mere thought of her embarking upon so perilous a quest. "To hunt them blindly, without knowledge, would be to risk life, and more than life, but I have hopes that soon there may come to Plymouth one who does possess such knowledge."

"Who?" Roxanne asked bluntly. "And why do you suppose he will come?"

"His name is Tobias Swinlake, and I hope that he will come because nigh on a week ago I sent him word of what is happening here. He is a man of great learning, one who has probed deep into the mysteries of such evil as now surrounds us and has often been called upon to aid in the discovery of it. If any may come at the truth, it is he. I first met with him seven years ago in the north, at a time when that part of the realm was grievously troubled by witches, and since at that same time the malignants of those parts were rallying to Charles Stuart, it was deemed necessary to provide Mr. Swinlake with a military escort. I was put in command of it, and though I was little more than a lad, it pleased him to hold converse with me, and to discourse somewhat upon the subject of witches and their hell-taught arts. He is merciless in their pursuit, but I know that he has more than once saved a woman unjustly accused. I believe that he can save her ladyship."

"If he comes," Imelda whispered, and put out her hand to him. "Giles, will he? Dare we hope for such mercy?"

"If my message reached him, he will come, for I had the good fortune to be of service to him in the north, and he is not the man to forget," Giles replied with quiet conviction, taking her hand in his. He did not feel it necessary to explain that the service he had done Mr. Swinlake was the saving of that gentleman's life. "My only fear is that he may be from home, and though I charged my messenger most straitly not to pause until he places my letter in Mr. Swinlake's hands, he may have to journey far to find him. As to that, we can only wait, and hope, and pray."

When Giles left the Dower House an hour or so later, Imelda walked with him along the track as far as the edge of the wood. That the servants would remark this, and Rebecca Moone, at least, find an opportunity to disclose it to Sir Darrell, she had no doubt, but a certain recklessness had taken possession of her now where Giles was concerned. It was impossible to know when they would meet again, and though he was putting the Conyngtons even more deeply in his debt, Imelda could place no dependence upon Sir Darrell being influenced by that consideration where her future was concerned. In her own heart and mind there were no doubts at all; she would gladly entrust that future to Giles's keeping, but she knew that the chance of her ever being permitted to do so was slight indeed.

When they reached the fringe of the woodland, Giles halted. The sun had dipped below the level of the trees, so that though the topmost boughs were still fretted with golden light, below the shadows clustered thickly, and reached out far across the rough grassland towards the house.

"No farther," he said firmly. "I will not let you walk alone through the woods at dusk. In truth"—he hesitated—"while this present trouble lasts I would not have you go out of sight of the house at any time unless you are well attended. You are placed here between those bigots in the village and Mrs. Shenfield's servants at the Moat House, and a measure of caution is needful."

He would not speak of his greatest fear for her, would scarcely acknowledge it even to himself, although it lurked constantly and agonizingly in the far recesses of his mind. Lady Conyngton had been accused of witchcraft; Imelda had recently been brought here to be her ladyship's close companion; how long would it be before the cry of "witch" was raised against Imelda herself? If it were, would the people of Conyngton be as reluctant to believe in her guilt as in that of their squire's lady, or would they seize eagerly upon it, and try to shift the whole blame on to her, the stranger, the newcomer?

He looked at her, slight and defenceless and inexpressibly dear, and for the first time in his life hated his chosen profession, and the duties of his military rank that must take him from her. Were he not a soldier, he could carry her out of danger now, tonight; take her far away from this devil-haunted village to the safety of his father's house in Bristol; marry her in defiance of her family and their accursed Royalist pride. Yet even as the thought passed through his mind, he knew that, were it possible, she would not go. Would not abandon the charge entrusted to her, or break the promise she had given Lady Conyngton, any more than he could desert from the army.

"You *will* be prudent?" he prompted her, speaking gently because he feared that to be too insistent would only add to her burden of anxiety. "Nothing will be gained by risking the sort of unpleasantness you may encounter if you venture abroad."

"Tomorrow is the Sabbath," she reminded him. "I must go to church."

"You must, but do not linger in the village, and keep the servants close about you while you are there.

If you can be all the time in Mrs. Pennan's company, so much the better."

"I will, I promise you, though I wish——!" She broke off abruptly, biting her lip.

"Wish what, my heart?"

"That you could be here, in Conyngton," she whispered, "instead of in Plymouth."

"I, also," he agreed with a touch of grimness. "A dozen of my troopers posted here, and you would see a speedy end to wayside preaching and rabble-rousing."

She did not doubt it, but she had been too long accustomed to think of the Ironside army as the enemy, the terrible engine of destruction that had shattered the Royalist cause and murdered the King, to look upon it now as an instrument of deliverance. It was Giles she wanted to keep within reach; he alone in whom her trust and dependence were placed.

"Will you be able to come again?" she asked wistfully.

"As soon as may be, I promise you, but I must bide in Plymouth until Swinlake comes, or sends me word. But you shall have news of what passes there, even if I cannot bring it myself."

"I shall be grateful for it. That is the hardest part, to wait, not knowing, wondering whether her danger be greater now, or less. And, Giles, if it were possible to get a message to her, to tell her that all is well here——!"

"I will do my best. No doubt it would ease her mind a little, poor lady, to know that." He was silent for a moment, fighting an unwillingness to leave her which was more than the mere reluctance of a lover to part from the beloved, but rather a growing conviction that grave danger threatened her. "You know now where a messenger may find me. If you have need of me, send word and I will come."

"I think I will always have need of you," she replied with a catch in her voice. "Oh, Giles—!"

He uttered a low-voiced exclamation and drew her a few paces further into the shadows beneath the trees, loping his horse's bridle over a low branch so that he might take her in his arms. Yet even the gladness and the wonder of it, of knowing that their love transcended for her, as it did for him, all the differences of birth and loyalty and tradition which stood between them, was darkened by that sense of lurking peril. Wild thoughts flashed through his mind; a crazy impulse to ride off with her now, abandoning duty and honour alike, for what mattered either compared with Imelda's safety? So compelling was the desire, and so close did he feel himself to succumbing to it, that he put her from him almost roughly.

"I must go now," he said hoarsely. "If I do not—!" He mastered his feelings with an effort, afraid that he had hurt or frightened her. After a moment he took her hands in his, palms upward, and pressed a kiss to each in turn. "Go back, my love," he said more calmly. "I will wait here until you reach the house."

She hesitated, looking searchingly at him through the gathering darkness, and then rose on tiptoe and reached up to kiss him again, lightly and swiftly, before drawing her hands from his. Next moment she was gone, running back towards the waiting house.

Giles stood watching the pale glimmer of her dress

until she reached the forecourt, saw her pause there
and turn for one backward look, and then he mounted
his horse and rode slowly away beneath the trees,
knowing that it was the only possible thing to do, yet
burdened still by that chill certainty that he was abandoning her to some nameless danger.

Imelda walked slowly down the stairs from the
nursery, frowning in troubled thought. Little Anne was
still fretful, and though Roxanne maintained stoutly
that the baby was troubled by nothing more serious
than a tooth agrowing, Imelda could not rid her mind
of nagging uneasiness. Her responsibility for the children's welfare weighed heavily upon her, and she was
haunted by a morbid dread that some mischance
would befall them during their parents' absence.

She had kept her promise to Giles, and stayed close
to the house except for the necessary visit to the
village church on Sunday. It was an experience she
had no desire to repeat. Dr. Malperne had returned
briefly from Plymouth to conduct the service, but the
strangers were still much in evidence, and one of
them had actually leapt to his feet during the sermon
to denounce "the Conyngton hag and her vile trafficking with the powers of Hell" in terms which had driven
the colour from Imelda's face and left her, and Roxanne who was with her, staring at each other in horror
and dismay, thankful for the high, panelled walls of
the squire's pew which hid them from the rest of the
congregation. After the service the villagers had scattered hurriedly and in sullen, fearful silence, to the
shelter of their homes, but Imelda caught a glimpse

of Daniel Stotewood, and was sickened by the look of savage triumph in his gaunt, unprepossessing face.

One slight shred of comfort had come today, with the knowledge that Sir Darrell was back in Devon at last. Soon after noon, Barnaby had arrived at the Dower House, to describe how he had sought out his master in London; of the desperate, breakneck journey back across the breadth of England; of Sir Darrell riding successive horses to a standstill and having to be almost forcibly restrained by his companions— Barnaby himself and his personal servant, John Parrish—in order to take the barest necessities of food and rest. He and Parrish had gone straight to Plymouth, leaving Barnaby to carry news of their return to the anxious household. Imelda could only pray that her kinsman's anxiety for his beloved wife, and his fury against her accusers, would not betray him into dangerous rashness once the city was reached.

Her thoughts returned to the ailing baby, and on a sudden impulse she decided to consult Charity's great book of "receipts," in which were inscribed remedies and potions dating back more than a hundred years. Her ladyship, so she had told Imelda, had found the book already at the Dower House, brought there, no doubt, by some former widowed Lady Conyngton when she removed from the great mansion on the hill. It was kept, together with the more costly oils and cordials, in a cupboard in the stillroom which was known as "her ladyship's cabinet," since Charity alone possessed a key to it, but this was of course, in the bunch which hung now from Imelda's waist.

As soon as the thought of the book occurred to

her, she hurried to the stillroom, and was relieved to find it empty, for she half expected Rebecca would be there. Unlocking the cupboard, she lifted the heavy leather-bound volume from its place, and as she did so, some small object wrapped in black velvet, which had apparently been tucked behind it, toppled forward and rolled to the edge of the shelf. Laying the book aside, she picked the thing up to restore it to its place, then, her curiosity aroused by the odd, irregular shape of it, unfolded the covering. Inside was a little figure of baked clay some inches long; it was roughly fashioned, but not so roughly that it was not instantly recognizable as the image of a child, a naked child with a scrap of pale yellow wool to represent its hair, and three long, sharp pins driven deep into its abdomen.

The room rocked and darkened around Imelda, there was a roaring sound in her ears, and when she came to herself again she was crouched on the bench by the table, sick and trembling with shock, with the horrible little image still clutched in her hand. She stared at it, resisting an impulse to cast it from her as something unclean. It could not be true. It could not, and yet here was evidence that could not be denied. A witch's image of little Jonathan Shenfield, who had died in agony, suddenly and mysteriously, screaming of "burning knives in his belly."

After a minute or two she laid the thing down on the bench and dragged herself to her feet, going reluctantly to peer again into the dark recess of the cupboard; seeing other objects there; thrusting in a shrinking hand and pulling out, first, a small jar of evil-smelling ointment, and then a half-burned candle made of black tallow. She put them on the bench beside the clay figure, and, dropping to her knees, prayed for guidance, for strength and courage to face the implications of her discovery and to do whatever had to be done.

Gradually she grew calmer, and was able to bring herself to look again at the vile evidence of witchcraft and murder that lay before her. Looking, she began to feel puzzled. On the face of it, only Charity herself could have hidden it in the cupboard, but what folly, to leave it so imperfectly concealed. True, she had the only key, but she had left that with Imelda, when she was taken to face the very charges of which these things provided damning proof. Besides, the malefic image had long since done its fatal work; would it not have been prudent to destroy it, rather than leave it where it could be discovered by the most cursory search?

As thought of a search came into her mind, so, too, came a memory, and she was standing again in the hall after Charity had been taken away, with Rebecca Moone speaking insolently of the Major's kindness for Imelda which had caused him to refrain from ordering a search of the house. She saw again the fury in the woman's face, heard it in her voice, and knew beyond all doubt that it had not, as she had supposed, been caused by Charity's arrest, but by the fact that the event had not followed the usual violent pattern of a witch-hunt. Rebecca had expected the house to be searched, and had somehow found the means to hide the image and other things in Charity's private cupboard in a deliberate attempt to convict her.

Rebecca was one of the witches, probably even the chief among them. Why had no one suspected her? Her recent arrival in the parish; her horrifying looks, her solitary habit of roaming abroad by day and night, ostensibly to seek herbs and plants for the stillroom. All these things should have aroused suspicion, and yet even Dr. Malperne had never pointed a finger in her direction. Imelda herself had not suspected it, in spite of the dread the woman inspired in her, but now, as though she had been granted a revelation, she was completely certain of Rebecca's guilt.

Kneeling still beside the bench, she tried to probe the mystery. Why had Rebecca sought to destroy her benefactress? Did a witch, being pledged to the Prince of Darkness, always return evil for good, so that Rebecca had rejoiced in the opportunity for wickedness offered by the situation between the Conyngtons and the Shenfields? Was she, by sowing the seeds of death and destruction in a hitherto peaceful community, carrying out the malevolent will of her Satanic master? The questions were unanswerable, but of two things, at least, Imelda had no doubt at all. She must send word to Giles, and she must dispose of the hideously dangerous evidence she had found.

Getting up from her knees, she stumbled on numb, cramped limbs to the cupboard, made sure there was nothing she had overlooked, and then replaced the book and locked the door. Then, thrusting the jar of ointment into her pocket, and remembering as she did so that the witches were said to anoint themselves with some magic unguent which gave them the power to fly, she wrapped the image and the candle in the piece of velvet and went cautiously out of the room.

To her relief she encountered no one as she hurried to her bedchamber and concealed her find beneath some clothing in one of the big oak chests there. Presently she would decide how to dispose of it, but, more urgent even than that, was the need to summon Giles to her aid.

She was prudent enough not to set down in writing any word of the things she had found, since if such information fell into the wrong hands it might damn Charity beyond all hope of acquittal, but she told him her suspicions of Rebecca Moone and begged him to come to Conyngton as soon as he could. Then she sent for Barnaby.

"I want you to carry this letter with all speed to Major Bradwell in Plymouth," she told him, "and then do whatever he bids you. He may wish to speak with Sir Darrell, so tell him where he may be found." She saw disapproval in the servant's eyes as he took the letter, and added sharply: "It is for her ladyship's sake, Barnaby. Believe me, the Major is very much our friend."

He looked unconvinced, but assured her that he would perform his errand as speedily as he could. He hurried from the room, and presently she saw him riding rapidly along the track towards the road. Heartened by the knowledge that her message was now on its way, Imelda turned her attention to the problem of disposing of her dangerous find.

She soon realized that this would not be easy. Her first thought had been to drop the things down the well but who could tell what poisonous substances the evil-looking ointment might contain? The river would serve equally as well, but the winding course of the stream was such that to reach its nearest point she would have to leave the park, walk some way along the road and then follow a patch which would bring her uncomfortably close to the village. She remembered Giles's warning, and felt she could not face the risk of encountering anyone hostile to the Conyngtons. If she were stopped, with those things in her possession—her mind shuddered away in horror from the thought.

Where, then? Where could she dispose of them where they would not be found, or she seen doing it? By this time she was in her own room again, with the incriminating objects retrieved from the chest, and with them clutched in her hands she walked distractedly across to the window and stood looking out; and found her answer.

Her room was at the back of the house, and she could see, beyond garden and orchard, the parkland rising in a long, tree-scattered slope to the wall behind which the ruins of the burned-out mansion brooded amid derelict gardens. Surely the crumbling walls and tangled greenery would offer a score of hiding places where a small bundle might lie lost and forgotten?

No sooner did the idea occur to her than she was acting upon it. She found a long, soft scarf, that Charity had given her, and wrapped the bundle in it, leaving the ends floating loose so that it looked as though she was merely carrying the scarf over her arm. Then she went down, and out into the garden, where she strolled idly along the paths as if taking the air, but making her way steadily towards the orchard, on the far side of which a stile gave access to the park between the Dower House and Conyngton itself.

Once beyond the stile she allowed herself to walk more purposefully, anxious to be rid of her sinister burden as soon as possible. Once that was disposed of, it would not matter if she encountered anyone, since there was no reason why she should not walk in the park if she wished to, but she had no real expectation of meeting anyone. Even by daylight, the villagers avoided the immediate vicinity of the ruins, and suddenly and uncomfortably Imelda remembered why. She found herself wishing she had not listened to the tales the servants whispered about the place.

She was quite close now to the wall which encircled the gardens. It loomed above her, crumbling away in places, patched with moss, and with weeds that had found a foothold amid the rotting mortar; trees thrust untamed branches above it, and ivy had climbed and spread across the bricks. A little to her right, the arch of the square Tudor gatehouse gaped like a toothless mouth.

Reluctantly she went towards it, telling herself firmly that there was nothing to fear, that ghosts and witches belonged to the darkness of night and not to a warm and golden evening, with the sinking sun painting long shadows across the grass, and swallows dipping and circling overhead. To the chill and stench of the charnel-house rather than the lush sweetness of high summer, with the scent of a hundred different flowers heavy on the breathless air.

She was hot and panting from her hurried walk up the hill, her clothes clinging damply to her in the sultry heat, but as she passed under the arch of the gatehouse a little shiver shook her, a chill which was of the spirit rather than of the flesh. Then she was through the archway and standing in the weed-grown forecourt; standing and staring, gripped by horror of a different kind.

It was hard to believe that this had ever been a human habitation of any sort, much less a great house giving shelter to scores of people. A stillness as of death brooded over it. On the opposite side of the forecourt a broad flight of steps led up to a terrace, and to what had once been the great door of the mansion, but which was now no more than another yawning hole, through which could be glimpsed the desolation beyond. The jagged, broken walls, half smothered in greenery, even with young trees thrusting through them; the ground between littered with shattered stone and blackened, rotting timbers; with fallen branches and drifts of withered leaves. On either side, gardens had become an impenetrable wilderness, a tangle of weeds and briars scattered with flowers, once cultivated, which had reverted to the wild, and of trees draped and smothered in curtains of climbing plants.

Timidly Imelda went forward, treading softly, for the smallest sound seemed loud in that death-like hush. Across the forecourt and up the steps to the house, picking her way between fragments of stone, some of which, here, bore half-obliterated traces of the familiar coat-of-arms of the Conyngtons. In the roofless, open space which must once have been the great hall she hesitated again, looking about her, and then made her way cautiously to a pile of stone in a far corner. There she unwrapped the bundle and poked the candles and the jar deep into cavities between the stones. Then she shrouded the clay image once more in its velvet wrapping, and beat and ground it to fragments with a heavy lump of stone before thrusting it, too, into one of the holes, pushing it, and the other things, far out of sight with a stick.

At last she rose to her feet and stood for a few moments looking down. Not a trace of the evidence of witchcraft remained. Falling leaves would drift over its hiding place, and snow softly cover it, and in season the green, growing things would come again, binding the stones yet closer together, burying the secret even deeper in this lost and forgotten place.

She was casting the scarf about her shoulders when a whisper of sound sent her swinging round, and out of the corner of her eye, as she turned, she thought she glimpsed a movement on the terrace. For a space she stood, staring with dilated eyes towards the doorway, her heart thumping and her throat suddenly dry with fear. Intent upon her task of concealment, she had not noticed that the sun had set, but now she realized that though the cloudless sky was still awash with light, it was light that deepened perceptibly from gold to rose, while the desolation about her had become a mystery of thickening shadows. And then there came again that tiny sound, like a stealthy footfall on cracked and broken stone.

With a gasp of fright Imelda started towards the doorway, hurrying now, stumbling in her haste to be away from these haunted ruins and out into the open parkland. She gained the terrace and saw, across the width of the forecourt, a hurrying, shambling figure disappear into the arch of the gatehouse.

She checked, staring in horrified dismay, not certain whether the thing she had seen was ghost or mortal but knowing with a tremor of dread that she must pass the same way to reach the park. She glanced frantically to right and left, but the wall, and the tangled wilderness of undergrowth, made any other path impossible; so she went forward again, slowly and reluctantly, each step a conscious effort towards the archway.

Suppose it were still there, lurking in the shadows under the arch, waiting for her? When she reached the gatehouse she paused again, peering fearfully along the length of the archway to the blessed sanity of the park beyond; and then she heard it, from somewhere on her left; the hurried, rasping breathing that sounded even more terrified than her own.

It was so intensely human a sound that much of her panic subsided. She looked for its source, and discovered something she had not noticed on her way in. There was a doorway in the wall of the archway, and it was from beyond this that the sound was coming. She crept forward and looked inside.

It was a small, bare room, no doubt the one-time quarters of the gatekeeper, and almost in darkness because a piece of sacking had been hung across the one small window, but Imelda could just make out a huddled figure in the farthest corner. A little gasp of fright broke from it as she appeared in the doorway and the sound emboldened her yet further so that she could find the courage to go forward and jerk the covering from the window to let in the fast fading daylight.

A scarecrow figure stared back at her. A girl, dirty, ragged and unkempt, peering up at Imelda between matted elf-locks of flaxen hair. She had been pretty once, but now her face was white and haggard, with dark shadows about the eyes, and her body heavy and clumsy with pregnancy.

"Matty Weddon!" Imelda said blankly. "Heaven protect us! Have you been hiding here ever since you ran away?"

There was no answer. Matty continued to peer up at her like some trapped and frightened animal, and something in the stare of the wild, blue eyes disquieted Imelda. She said very gently:

"Don't be afraid, Matty. I'll not harm you."

The tangled head was shaken, the blue gaze never shifting from her face. Matty said in a hoarse whisper:

"You'll tell where I be. They'll take and hang me for a witch."

This seemed all too likely. If Matty's whereabouts were discovered, the mere fact that she had managed to survive during the weeks since her disappearance by hiding in the reputedly haunted ruins would alone be enough to prove her guilt to the satisfaction of most people; and yet. . . .

"You cannot stay here, Matty, not for much longer,"

Imelda pointed out gently. "Not when the time comes for your baby to be born. You will need help then."

A look of cunning flickered in Matty's eyes. "I'll lack for naught. Meanwhile 'tis safe here, as long as none but us knows on't."

"Us?" Imelda repeated sharply.

She looked around, realizing for the first time that bare though the room was, some attempt had been made to furnish it. Matty crouched on blankets on a rough straw pallet; there were a couple of stools, and platters and mugs and other domestic utensils; far more than the girl could have carried with her when she fled from her home.

"The coven," Matty said, and chuckled. "One brought one thing, one another. They take it by turns to feed me. Her told 'em to do it. Her brought me here, when her found me at Tabby's after I fled from Father."

Imelda was conscious of a little chill of fear. So Matty really was a member of the witch-coven, as Tabitha had been, and her fellow witches had been hiding and caring for her all these weeks, commanded to it by—whom? Imelda knew the answer to that question even before she asked it.

"*Who* brought you here, Matty?"

"Rebecca," the girl answered simply. "Mistress o' the coven, her be."

Imelda waited to hear no more. All her suspicions had been confirmed, and she must waste no time in getting away. She wondered whether Matty would try to prevent her from leaving. Imelda was closer to the doorway, and could be through it before the other girl had heaved herself to her feet, and there was little doubt that she could outdistance any pursuit down the hill, even if Matty were not afraid to emerge from the ruins. True, the girl was a witch, and might command unknown forces, and yet Imelda felt instinctively that her powers were not great. She was too simple a creature for that.

Keeping her gaze on the girl, she withdrew a cautious pace towards the doorway, and then another, and another. Matty had not moved. From her place on the pallet she peered up through her tangled hair, and there was no longer any fear in the bright, blue eyes. Imelda turned to make her escape, only to recoil with a cry of terror. Framed in the doorway, impassive yet menacing, stood Rebecca Moone herself.

Imelda shrank back, cowering as though from a threatened blow, and yet Rebecca had not moved. She stood with folded arms, a neat, incongruous figure in that setting, with her plain dark gown and snowy cap and apron and broad collar, incongruous, that is, until one looked at her face; at the chilling contrast between the gaunt, handsome features of one side and the horrifying, grotesque distortion of the other. Until one looked into her eyes.

Once again Imelda was gripped by the terror which had seized her when she and Giles came face to face with Rebecca in the wood, but this time it was utterly overwhelming. This time Rebecca did not turn away, but continued steadily to regard her, so that her mind and her will were held captive, helpless and shuddering, by the power of those glittering, silver-coin eyes. With what seemed to be an enormous effort, as though the limb was encased in lead, Imelda raised her right arm and stretched out her hand in the gesture which was supposed to give protection against witchcraft. A slight, contemptuous smile touched Rebecca's twisted mouth and she took a deliberate pace forward.

Try as she would, Imelda could not look away from those terrible eyes. She drew back a pace as the woman took another step towards her, and even though her gaze was trapped and held, it seemed that she could see, around and above Rebecca, a darkness that moved as she moved. A sense of indescribable evil filled the little room as steadily and without lifting a finger, the witch-woman drove Imelda back from the door.

At length her back was against the opposite wall and she could retreat no further, but still Rebecca came on. A little, whimpering sound of pure terror broke from Imelda's lips and she covered her face with her hands, but an instant later bony fingers gripped her wrists and her hands were forced apart and down. The horribly scarred face and glittering eyes, seeming to float, disembodied, in a cold, black mist, were within an inch or two of her own, and she was defenceless before a horror that seemed to rise straight from Hell itself. Her senses gave way before it, and she knew no more.

When she came to herself again, she was lying on a rough, evil-smelling blanket, unable to move, and after the first moment of panic it was almost a relief to realize that this helplessness was due to something as mundane as being bound hand and foot. She felt sick and dizzy, and a little time passed before she grasped the fact that she was still in the gatehouse, on the pallet which served Matty Weddon as a bed. She lay on her side, facing the wall, against which the hump of her own shadow was etched by a feeble glimmer of candlelight coming from somewhere behind her.

When she felt a little stronger, she heaved herself over on to her back and turned her head to look across the room. The candle stood on one of the two stools, and on the other Matty was sitting, eating from a wooden bowl held in her lap. Of Rebecca Moone there was now no sign.

Imelda's movement drew the other girl's glance towards her, but Matty said nothing and merely went on unconcernedly with her meal. Looking past her, Imelda saw that the curtain of sackcloth was in place again across the window, so, with the doorway sunk deep in the arch of the gatehouse, there was no risk of any gleam of light being seen beyond the wall.

She wondered how long her swoon had lasted, and, fearfully, what Rebecca intended towards her. It seemed beyond all doubt that her life would be forfeited, for the witch-coven would show no mercy, and she dared not let herself speculate upon the horrific guise death might assume. Her only chance lay in escape or rescue.

The hope of either seemed frighteningly remote. Even if Giles came at once in response to her letter, he would find her gone from the Dower House and have no idea where to look for her; or, for that matter, for Rebecca Moone. Where *was* Rebecca? Was she even now, elsewhere in the ruins, concocting some horrible spell against her latest victim? Crouching over an image of clay, perhaps, or muttering incantations above some hellish brew?

Imelda told herself resolutely that she must not think about Rebecca. That way panic lay, and panic would rob her forever of any slight chance of survival that might still exist. She looked again at Matty; saw her put down the empty bowl, wipe the back of her hand across her mouth, and then pick up a mug which stood on the floor beside her and drink deeply.

Watching her, Imelda realized that she was herself parched with thirst. She said faintly:

"Matty! Matty, if you have any pity in you, give me a drink."

For a moment the girl looked at her. Then she got up and came to kneel clumsily beside the pallet, to raise Imelda's head and hold the mug to her lips. It was still half full of the sweet Devon cider which was the country folk's commonest drink, and after swallowing a little Imelda was able to say more clearly:

"Thank you, Matty. Will you help me to sit up?" She saw distrust in the girl's eyes, and added pleadingly: "Please, I beg of you! It hurts intolerably to lie like this, with my hands tied behind me."

After another hesitation, Matty put down the mug and hauled her prisoner up into a sitting position, helping her to get her back against the wall. The movement made Imelda's head swim again; she rested it against the rough brickwork behind her and willed the dizziness to pass, dimly hearing Matty remark stolidly:

" 'Twont be for long."

The words struck Imelda with a little chill of foreboding, and as soon as the room had stopped spinning around her, she opened her eyes again and looked at her companion, who had returned to her former place on the stool.

"Why are you keeping me prisoner here? What do you intend?"

Matty shook her head. "That be'ant for me to say. Rebecca told me to keep watch on you till her comes back."

"She has gone?" Imelda tried to keep the relief from her voice. "Whither?"

"Back to the Dower House. I don't know for why."

Imelda thought, "But I know. It will not do for us both to be absent without any explanation, and Rebecca will want to know if a search is being made for me, and where. Perhaps even to send it on a false trail."

So if she were to have any hope of escape, the attempt must be made soon, while the most dangerous adversary was out of the way. If she could only get free, it would not be difficult to evade Matty and to hurry across the park, not to the Dower House, but to Roxanne. They could set someone at the gate to watch for Giles. . . .

Stealthily she tested the bonds about her wrists, watching the other girl from beneath her lashes as she did so. Matty sat staring vacantly before her, rocking gently to and fro on the stool with her arms clasped about her swollen abdomen, and apparently paying no heed at all to her prisoner. Imelda struggled harder, wrenching and twisting at the cords, but though they bit painfully into her flesh, they did not give in the least; if anything, they seemed tighter than before, and gradually the certainty forced itself upon her that escape did not lie that way.

How, then? She looked again at Matty, thinking that, witch though the girl undoubtedly was, she did not seem particularly ill-disposed. She was certainly a simple, good-natured creature, easily imposed upon, and though she was undoubtedly in awe of Rebecca Moone, it might be possible to win her confidence, perhaps even her help.

"Matty," she said gently, "tell me how you came to this evil of witchcraft. Was it through Tabitha Spragge?"

The blue, somehow disturbing eyes turned slowly towards her. Matty shook her head.

"Nay." There was a hint of scorn in the reply. "Tabby had small power, save for herbs and simples and suchlike. Her said her could scry, but 'tweren't true."

"Scry?" Imelda repeated. "You mean look into the future?"

"Aye. Her tried, time and again, with a bit o' mirror, and with ink in a bowl, but her never told us aught as meant anything. Then Rebecca came."

"And Rebecca *can* scry?" Imelda prompted softly as Matty paused.

"Aye, if her wants to, but that be'ant all. Her be a witch o' great power—*you've* learned that by now— and her said her would lead us, and teach us, if so be us'd follow her, and give ourselves to *her* Master, the true Prince o' the World."

"Rebecca's master is the Devil," Imelda reminded her sternly, and Matty nodded.

"Aye," she agreed calmly, "so *you'd* call him. To us he's our Master."

"Matty, why?" Imelda asked blankly. "Why did you, and the other women, let Rebecca trick you into such wickedness and evil?"

Matty scowled, looking at once sullen and perplexed as she tried to find words with which to explain. "It weren't no trick. Besides, there ought to be summat more than work from morn till night, and preaching o' Hell-fire and damnation all day Sunday. Maybe 'twere different in the old days, when it weren't no sin to be mirthful, but now there be no bearing it."

"And is this better? Hiding here like a hunted animal, afraid to show your face lest you be taken for a witch?"

" 'Twon't be for long." Matty was wholly sullen now. "Rebecca says so."

"Rebecca is lying. Matty, there is a child murdered, and Mrs. Shenfield and your father lying close to death. And Lady Conyngton imprisoned in Plymouth, accused of crimes which you and the rest of your coven have committed. Do you feel no remorse at all?"

"I be sorry for her ladyship," Matty admitted slowly. "Her be no witch, and her were always kind to me."

"Then let me go. Untie me, and come with me to Mrs. Pennan's house. We will keep you safe, and send word to Plymouth, and when it is known you have confessed in order to save Lady Conyngton, no harm will come to you." Imelda had an uneasy feeling that she was making promises which could never be fulfilled, but she reminded herself that Matty was undoubtedly guilty, and that it was her life against Imelda's own, and Charity's, and possibly others, too, since if the witches were taken, the spell might perhaps be broken, and Elizabeth Shenfield and the smith recover. "Matty, I beg of you! It is the only way you can make amends."

Matty shook her head. "I dursn't, even if I wanted to."

"And you do not want to?"

"Nay! Why should I? You be naught to me, nor Mrs. Shenfield neither, and as for my father, I be glad he's stricken. He beat me so cruel that last time I could scarce crawl as far as Tabby's. Let him rot!"

There was sudden venom in her voice, and Imelda remembered Abigail Bramble telling her how Matty had screamed curses at her father as he whipped her. Had curses been followed by more potent incantations? Had an image been made of Weddon also, and used to call down upon him the worst thing that could befall a man of active life and great physical strength? She shivered, for there was something particularly horrible in the thought of the girl practising the black arts against her own father. If she was capable of that, what hope was there of moving her to pity?

She shifted her position against the wall, and once more strained at her bonds, but to no avail. Matty appeared to have forgotten her again. Imelda watched her rise heavily from the stool and stretch herself, one hand pressed to the small of her back. The shadow of her thickened body loomed grotesquely across the wall behind her, and suddenly another thought flashed into Imelda's mind. Matty cared nothing for the fate of her father; was she equally indifferent about her unborn child?

"Matty," she said urgently, "what of your baby? No matter what you have done, the child is innocent and should not be made to suffer. If it is born here, with no one but Rebecca and the other witches to help you, it is damned even before it draws its first breath. They will pledge the babe to Satan—!"

She broke off, shocked into silence, for Matty had turned again to face her, and, incredibly, Matty was laughing. Softly and horribly, in a way which somehow conjured up a faint echo of the evil that had filled the room while Rebecca Moone was there.

"Fool!" The malevolent, sneering whisper, unlike Matty's ordinary tones, was evil, too, and so was the glittering gaze fixed upon Imelda. "Fools, the whole pack of 'ee. Didn't I tell 'ee, time and again, I've lain wi' no man? Pledge the babe to my Master? No need, for 'twas him as fathered it."

"The Devil?" Imelda's flesh seemed to crawl with horror. It was known that many witches had confessed to carnal knowledge of the Fiend, and had not Dr. Malperne made some such accusation against Matty? He had spoken also of the powers of Hell walking alive upon the earth, but until this moment the phrase had meant nothing to Imelda. Now, suddenly, with Matty's sneering, triumphant face, it became real; vividly, horribly real.

"Aye, the Devil!" There was pride as well as triumph in the girl's voice. "Of all the coven, I be the chosen one, the only one he's got wi' child. That's why they must keep me safely hid, and tend me till the babe be born. I'll have power then, the power and the knowledge, same as Rebecca. Her told me so."

Imelda closed her eyes, shutting out the sight of Matty's face, which somehow was now the face of a stranger. Her mind was still reeling from the shock of what she had been told. Either the girl was mad, driven out of her mind by witchcraft and by the privations she had undergone, or—but the alternative was too terrible to contemplate. The Devil made flesh; the Fiend incarnate, stalking the woods and meadows of Conyngton St. John, called forth from Hell by the evil powers of the woman with the scarred face and eyes like silver coins. It could not be true. Nothing would make her believe it.

" 'Ee don't believe me!" The hissing whisper came again, uncannily answering her secret thoughts. "But 'ee will, me dear! 'Ee will! The coven meets tonight. It be Lammas Eve, and he'll come to us, our Master, the Horned One. Ye'll see, and believe afore he passes judgement on 'ee."

The moon had risen, and was riding full and high in the cloudless sky. Imelda, alone now in the gate-house, could tell that this was so because, even with the sacking across it, the window showed faintly luminous, a lighter patch against the darkness in which she had been left when the candle guttered out. Matty had gone long since, hurrying out when the first foot-steps pattered softly through the archway, but there had been others after that, and a mutter of voices and an occasional smothered laugh. The witch-coven was assembling to do homage to its Satanic master, and Imelda sat alone in the darkness, sick and chilled with terror of what lay ahead.

There was no hope of escape. Her body ached in every muscle from the cramped immobility of the past few hours, while the cords tight about wrist and ankle had robbed the extremities of her limbs of feeling, so that even if the bonds had been suddenly and miraculously loosened she would have been incapable of flight. Matty had failed her. In spite of her undoubted good nature and quite genuine regret over Charity's plight, she was as arrant a witch as Rebecca Moone herself, glorying in her witchhood and in the alleged seed of Hell she carried in her womb. There was no hope, and Imelda, in her dread of what was to come, had begun to wish that the waiting would end, before panic robbed her of all self-control.

She realized suddenly that the voices and the footsteps had ceased. Silence had settled again over the ruins, but it was a silence charged with terror, as though the night itself was holding its breath in anticipation of the coming of some awful presence. She found that she was holding hers, too, her heart thudding until she felt it must choke her; and then the stillness was broken by a sound so unexpected, so incongruous at that time and place, that it had its own strange quality of horror.

It was the sound of a pipe, a recorder perhaps, or shepherd's pipe, playing a light and lilting tune. A tune to set the feet tapping; a tune to which to dance.

A merry sound, rising and falling, echoing eerily among the crumbling walls and roofless rooms of the once proud mansion; and, with the music and in time to it, the sound of feet on the cracked flagstones of the forecourt. Imelda, cowering back against the wall, could picture the witches whirling in a Hell-taught dance, with who could tell what demon partners? Faster and faster the music sounded, faster the dancing feet, and then, as suddenly as it had begun, the piping ceased.

In the smothering silence that succeeded it, Imelda became aware of a foul smell, a reeking, sulphurous stench that seemed to seep into the room through the open doorway, and as she gasped and choked from it, she heard someone speaking in the courtyard. The voice she recognized as Rebecca Moone's, although she could not make out the words, and then another voice replied; the deeper tones of a man, yet with a curiously hollow and muffled note that sounded scarcely human. Again the words were indistinguishable, but were clearly a command, and after a minute or so a glimmer of light brightened along the archway, and two women, one of them bearing a candle, came into the room.

Imelda shrank back as far as her bonds permitted, staring up at them in terror, seeing faces which were vaguely familiar but to which, in her present panic, she could put no names. One of the women knelt to unfasten the cords about her ankles, and then they hauled her to her feet, holding her up between them by gripping her bound arms, since her legs refused to support her.

In this fashion they dragged her out of the room and along the archway to the forecourt, flooded now with silver moonlight from end to end. Imelda, half fainting with dread, saw the other witches kneeling, motionless, in a semicircle facing the terrace steps; all save Rebecca, who stood erect, with folded arms, at one end of the line. At the foot of the steps, on either side, a fire had been kindled, fires which burned with an evil, bluish flame and sent forth reeking clouds of smoke that rose and spread sluggishly on the breathless air.

The smoke partially veiled the steps, and the figure, black-clad and with a voluminous black cloak spreading all about it, that sat upon the topmost stair, but as her captors dragged Imelda between their kneeling companions to the foot of the steps, she saw, through the drifting, sulphurous haze, that which sent her mind reeling from such an impact of disbelief that she doubted her own sanity. Above the folds of the cloak the moonlight gleamed on a long goat-face, on a coarse straggle of beard and the backward sweep of horns. On the ultimate horror, the obscenity of a beast's head crowning a human form.

Imelda's captors had no need to force her into an attitude of submission before the goat-headed thing, for when, at the foot of the steps, they ceased to hold her up, her legs buckled beneath her and only their hands still gripping her shoulders saved her from falling helplessly forward on to her face. After that one glimpse of the horror above her she did not dare to look up again, but crouched with bent head and stared down at the cracked flagstones on which she knelt, overwhelmed by a dread to which all her earlier fears were as nothing. She tried to pray, her mind seeming to grope in vain after the familiar words through the stinking fumes that lay like a fog over her brain.

Rebecca Moone spoke from her place at the witch-god's left hand. "You have pried into our secrets and looked upon that which only the coven may look upon and live, and yet we offer you mercy. We lack one of our number since she whom you knew as Tabitha was killed. Take her place. Swear allegiance to our Master, the Horned One, and your life will be spared."

"No!" Imelda's horrified whisper must have been inaudible two paces away; she realized it, and shook her head emphatically, without looking up. "No, I will not."

"Think on it," Rebecca's voice came again. "To refuse is to die, now, tonight, for you have seen our faces and we shall not let you live to denounce us. So join with us. Renounce your Christian faith and Christian baptism, submit yourself body and soul to our Master, who is the true Prince of the World, and once the pact be sealed he will grant you whatever you most desire. Power, or riches, or"—she paused, and when she spoke again her voice had sunk to a whisper, evil and insidious, as she bent close above the cringing girl—"or even a certain tall soldier to husband, if that is what you wish."

Despairingly Imelda shook her head. She seemed to be sinking into a black pit of horror; faintness was sweeping over her and she fought it frantically, dimly comprehending the bestialities which might be wrought upon her if she lay unconscious. Rebecca was speaking again, softly and compellingly.

"Look at me! You feel my power. You have always felt it, since first you looked into my eyes. You, and only you! You are not as these others, these ignorant clods. To you I can impart my secrets and my arts. Look at me now. Look into my eyes and learn of me. Look at me, Imelda. Look . . . at . . . me!"

The voice seemed to be speaking now in her own mind, and the urge to obey it was almost irresistible. With tight-closed eyes she tried to fight against it, knowing that once she looked into Rebecca's eyes she would be lost, damned beyond hope of salvation, enslaved by the hideous goat-headed presence on the steps above her. She was being dragged down into a vortex of horror; a soundless cry for help seemed to rise from the very depths of her being, and somehow, in the utmost extremity of her need, the plea was answered. Suddenly she found that she was praying aloud, gasping the words between trembling lips, and the awful hold upon her spirit was slowly loosening.

She heard Rebecca curse viciously, and then the woman's fingers twisted themselves into her hair, dragging her head savagely up and back, so that the sudden sharp pain jerked her abruptly into full awareness of her surroundings. Her eyes flew open, and she saw the creature on the steps rising slowly to its full height. It stretched out its arms, and a cold darkness seemed to envelope her as the cloak spread wide like gigantic wings. Helpless in the witches' grasp, unable to free herself from Rebecca's cruel hold, she stared up at the Satanic presence looming above her, dimly aware of a long, bright blade in one uplifted hand, but seeing only the goat-head of the Devil incarnate, horned and terrible against the moon.

Part 6

In the wainscoted parlour of an unpretentious inn in
Plymouth, Sir Darrell Conyngton sat alone, while the
evening shadows thickened around him as though they
were his own black despair made visible. His mission
to London had been more successful than he had
ever dared to hope, but just as he had been on the
point of setting out thankfully for home, Barnaby had
arrived with the unbelievable news that Charity had
been charged with practising witchcraft.

Since that moment, Darrell had been aware only of
the necessity of reaching Plymouth in the shortest
possible time, and of the fear that trial, sentence and
execution might follow one another in such quick
succession, that he might never see his wife again.
Not until that afternoon, when he once more held

her in his arms, had that dread been allayed, but now it was sweeping over him again. As yet she was unharmed, but she was still a prisoner facing one of the most dreadful charges that could be made against a woman. A charge which, if proved, would mean death by hanging.

The sound of the door being quietly opened did not rouse him, and only when his servant, John Parrish, spoke his name did he lift his head from his hands, blinking in the light of the candle the man carried. It was almost dark in the parlour now, for though the sky was still bright with sunset, the low ceiling, and the shadow of the tall house on the opposite side of the narrow street, brought darkness to it early.

"Sir," Parrish said apologetically, "Major Bradwell is below with another gentleman. They crave speech with your honour."

"Bradwell?" Darrell repeated dully. There was a pause, and then he brushed a hand across his eyes and spoke more decisively. "Yes, I must see him. Light the candles, John, and then bring the gentlemen to me."

When Giles and his companion came into the room he had risen to receive them, outwardly master of himself once more, but as they greeted each other Giles thought with swift compassion that Conyngton looked ten years older than at their last meeting. And how should he not, with his wife in such peril?

He introduced his companion as Tobias Swinlake. Sir Darrell greeted him courteously and invited him to be seated, but immediately turned again to Giles.

"I am in your debt, Major Bradwell," he said stiffly. "From Miss Hallett's letter, and even more from what

my wife told me today, I know how you exerted yourself to spare her."

"Bringing her ladyship to Plymouth, Sir Darrell, was
not a task I relished, believe me," Giles replied with
a touch of grimness, "but, since it had to be done,
it seemed to me necessary that I should be the one
to do it. You saw her today. Was there any difficulty
in arranging that?"

"None sought to prevent it," Darrell said, in a tone
which suggested it was as well that they had not. "She
has not, I thank God, been ill-used, except for that
damnable search they compelled her to agree to." His
voice shook, and he struck the table beside him with
his clenched fist. "That my wife should be so humili-
ated!"

"Yet since no witch-mark was found upon her,"
Mr. Swinlake put in mildly, "it is as well, sir, that the
search was made. Anything which helps to establish
her ladyship's innocence must be accepted, though not
necessarily welcomed."

Darrell directed towards him a haughty, challenging
look. Giles said quickly:

"Mr. Swinlake, Sir Darrell, is deeply learned in all
matters pertaining to witchcraft and the discovery
thereof. I had some acquaintance with him a few
years ago, and it is at my suggestion that he has come
to Plymouth."

Darrell glanced at him and then looked at Swinlake
again. He said angrily: "My wife is no witch! The
charge is false."

"I do not doubt it, sir," Swinlake agreed calmly.
"From what Major Bradwell had told me, malice is

not lacking in those who have accused her. Yet, though her ladyship be innocent of it, witchcraft is undoubtedly being practised in your unhappy parish."

"That is why Mr. Swinlake wishes to talk with you," Giles explained, "and why I brought him to you as soon as I learned of your arrival. You must know the village and those who live there better than any man."

"No doubt I do, but I would hesitate to hazard a guess as to who might be concerned in this foul evil, or for what reason."

"The malice of a witch, Sir Darrell, requires no such cause as you or I would need to bring us to a mortal quarrel," Swinlake reminded him gravely. "I remember, some years ago—!"

He paused, for Parrish had come back into the room. The servant looked apologetic, but there was a suggestion, too, of indignation in his manner as he said:

"Your pardon, Sir Darrell, but Dr. Malperne is here and urgent to speak with you. I told him your honour is engaged with company, but he grows importunate and will not take nay for an answer. What would you have me tell him?"

"Malperne here?" Darrell repeated incredulously, and then astonishment gave way to anger. "Upon my life, this is intolerable! First he accuses my wife of witchcraft, and then comes demanding to see me. Tell him to go hang himself!"

"A moment, Sir Darrell, by your leave," Mr. Swinlake broke in urgently. "One of her ladyship's accusers, say you? Then I pray you, have him come in. Let us hear what he has to say."

Darrell's angry glance rested briefly on the speaker and then passed to the tall young man in scarlet and steel who stood before the fireplace. Giles said quietly:

"I believe it were well to subdue your natural anger, sir, and have the preacher in. It had been my experience, and no doubt yours as well, that one can only benefit from knowing what the enemy is about. Besides"—with a touch of humour—"we can always cast him forth again if he offends beyond bearing."

For a moment longer Darrell continued to regard him, and then he nodded curtly to Parrish. When the servant returned with Dr. Malperne, it was obvious from the preacher's expression that he was surprised and not altogether pleased to discover the identity of the younger of Sir Darrell's visitors. He bowed stiffly, and said, with a meaning look at Conyngton:

"I had hoped, sir, to speak privately with you."

"You will speak to me in the presence of these gentlemen or not at all," Darrell informed him grimly. "In truth, I marvel that you have the insolence to approach me at all, matters standing as they do."

"I am here, Sir Darrell, because I conceive it to be my Christian duty, just as I felt it my duty to lay the facts of the recent dreadful happenings in Conyngton St. John before the Justices, and to support Mr. Taynton's accusations against her ladyship. Now, I confess to you, I am grievously troubled in my conscience."

"As well you may be, having placed an innocent woman in peril of her life." Darrell's voice shook with his consuming anger. "By God! Do you dare come prating to me—to *me*—of your conscience? Say what you have to say and then begone, before you try my patience beyond all bearing!"

"What troubles your conscience, Dr. Malperne?" Giles asked quietly. "Are you convinced now that Lady Conyngton was wrongfully accused?"

"That, Major, is not for me to determine," the preacher told him reprovingly. "Mrs. Shenfield accused her of bewitching the child to death, and then Mrs. Shenfield herself became the victim of a malefic spell. It was needful that her ladyship should be publicly accused of that in order that the truth may be established, but other charges have since been made against her, and one of them, at least, I know to be false, and prompted by malice."

"Damn you, Malperne, they are all false!" Darrell said furiously. "As false as Hell!"

Mr. Swinlake leaned forward to lay a restraining hand on his arm. "Patience, Sir Darrell! I think the good Doctor, at least, bears no grudge against your wife, but is prompted only by loathing of the evil he sees at work in his parish." He looked at Malperne. "Of which charges, sir, do you speak?"

The preacher looked resentfully at him, obviously wondering who he was and what business of his it might be. No one enlightened him, and he addressed his reply pointedly to Giles.

"There is no truth in Taynton's assertion that Lady Conyngton seduced his wife by witchcraft into her lover's arms. I was close in Jonas Shenfield's confidence for years, and I know, as others do, that the lewd, immodest passion Sarah Shenfield cherished for the malignant, Mordisford, sprang from nothing

more than common carnal desire. It was to save her
from the sin of yielding to the lusts of the flesh that
her brother arranged her marriage to Mr. Taynton,
and she resisted his commands by every means in her
power until the very eve of her wedding. When
Mordisford came to her again two years later her
ladyship may well have aided them in their flight—
indeed, she confessed to it—but she had no need to
use magical powers to persuade her cousin into
adultery."

"And Taynton knows it," Darrell agreed more
calmly. "He has never forgiven my wife for helping
her cousin to escape from his house, even though it
was his own harsh treatment as much as anything
that drove Sarah away. Now he has seized this opportunity to settle the score."

"And to win sympathy for himself in place of ridi-
cule," Giles added shrewdly, "since if a man's wife
is bewitched into cuckolding him, no blame can attach
to him." He looked again at Malperne, "So, sir, having
realized that one charge against Lady Conyngton is
false, have you begun to wonder whether the others
may be equally groundless?"

"It was then that I first began to doubt," Malperne
admitted. "I recalled that Mrs. Shenfield was at first
her ladyship's accuser, and that she has always disliked
her niece. Nor was there any recent quarrel between
them. I began to ask myself, as I had done at the time
of the child's death, whether the poor lady might be
mistaken. For Satan layeth cunning traps to trick the
Lord's elect into misdoing, and to protect those whom
he hath made his own. If her ladyship be wrongfully

accused, then the true culprits are still free to practise their hellish arts and to wreak further grievous harm."

"It is plain, sir, that you have good reason to be troubled," Mr. Swinlake said sympathetically. "If Lady Conyngton is wrongfully accused, then while you are obliged to linger here, supporting the false charges against her, those unhappy people whose spiritual well-being is in your care become the defenceless prey of the foul Fiend and his servants and followers upon earth."

Dr. Malperne was regarding him now with a more kindly eye. Who the stranger might be he did not know, but it was clear that he entered more completely into the Doctor's feelings than did either of his companions. His ready understanding was a welcome contrast to Conyngton's open hostility, and the sternness of the Major.

"You speak truth, sir," he agreed. "I am deeply conscious of their peril, and by my concern for them, and for those unfortunates already stricken, the Lord has seen fit to try my conscience yet further. As I prayed for them, that they may be delivered from their suffering, the thought came to me that this might be achieved by taking her ladyship back to Conyngton and into the presence of those whom the Devil has afflicted. For it is widely known, sir, as no doubt you are aware, that a spell may be broken if the victim draws blood from the witch above the breath."

This time it was Giles who moved, quickly and quietly, to set a hard, compelling grip on Darrell's shoulder, for Conyngton had already half risen from his seat, his face white with anger and with shock.

Giles was not surprised. The barbaric custom of allowing a supposed victim of enchantment to scratch or slash the face of the alleged witch above the level of the nostril was common enough, but he could well imagine Sir Darrell's feelings on hearing it proposed that this should be practised upon his wife. For a second or two the elder man furiously resisted the restraining hand, but then yielded to it, and to the warning in Giles's eyes.

"That suggestion finds no favour in your sight, Sir Darrell," Malperne observed dispassionately, "but consider that if this were done, and the spell remained unbroken, her ladyship's innocence would be established. And that, gentlemen, is the root of my disquiet, for when I spoke my thought to Mr. Taynton, he condemned it with unbecoming violence, and commanded me to speak of it to no one else. Yet surely, if he believes her ladyship justly accused, he ought to welcome that which would at the one time, prove her guilt and offer hope for her victims. That he welcomes it not suggests to me that he has no belief in her guilt, but makes his charges out of malice, and an unworthy and un-Christian desire to be avenged upon her for aiding his wife in her flight."

"And you, Dr. Malperne?" Swinlake questioned swiftly. "Do you believe Lady Conyngton innocent or guilty?"

"I have acted in good faith," the preacher replied stiffly, "and wait now for the charge to be proved or disproved. If her ladyship be found innocent, I will rejoice to see her safely restored to her family, for I bear her no personal ill-will, but the judgement is not for me to make."

Swinlake looked at Sir Darrell. "If it can be proved that your wife's foremost accuser is prompted by malice, the case against her will be greatly weakened. I believe that Dr. Malperne should make public declaration of his doubts, and the reason for them."

"But the risk!" Darrell said slowly. "If the Justices act upon this infamous suggestion, and take my wife, bound and helpless, into her aunt's presence, that she may draw blood——" He paused, appalled by the possibilities of such a situation. "No! I know Elizabeth Shenfield. She was half crazed before, and if she believes Charity to be the author of her present ills, who can tell what injury she may do her?"

"Such trial would be conducted with due care and propriety," Malperne informed him indignantly. "Mrs. Shenfield would be restrained—a scratch across the brow, no more."

"A small price to pay, sir," Mr. Swinlake pointed out, "to prove her ladyship innocent. It would be an impertinence for me to remind you of the danger in which she stands at present."

He broke off as the door opened. Darrell looked around impatiently, and then anxiety darkened his eyes as he saw Barnaby hesitating on the threshold. He rose quickly to his feet.

"You here? Is something amiss at home? Come in, man, and tell me!"

Barnaby came reluctantly into the room. "Miss Imelda sent me, your honour, with a letter." He hesitated, looking from one to the other.

"Then give it to me, in God's name!" Darrell stretched out an imperious hand. "Have your wits gone a-begging?"

Barnaby drew out the sealed letter, and then hesitated again. He looked acutely uncomfortable. "It be for Major Bradwell, your honour."

"What?" The word came explosively, and he was turning in angry suspicion when Giles stepped calmly forward.

"I took the liberty, Sir Darrell, of giving Miss Hallett my direction, and assuring her that I was at her service if there was further trouble of any kind." He held out his hand. "The letter, if you please."

Barnaby found himself unable to withstand the authority behind that pleasantly spoken request. He handed over the letter; Giles ripped it open and glanced rapidly down the hastily written page; a quick frown came.

"Miss Hallett believes she has discovered one of the witches." He held the letter out to Darrell. "A maidservant at the Dower House."

Darrell read the letter, his anger forgotten. "Rebecca Moone?" He paused, considering. "It is possible. She has been in our service a scant two years, and we know very little about her."

"I believe I saw her once," Giles said thoughtfully. "Is she not a tall woman, her face most horribly disfigured by a great scar?"

"What's that?" Tobias Swinlake rapped out the question in a voice that made them all start; a voice utterly unlike his previous mild tones. "A woman in her middle years, handsome once, but with the left side of her face hideously marred? Eyes of a strange, light grey?"

"That is she," Darrell agreed slowly. "We found her destitute and starving, and took her out of pity into our household. She is our stillroom maid, and greatly skilled in the art."

"Ask not where she learned her skill, or the uses she makes of it," Swinlake said heavily. He looked shaken. "Sir Darrell, when you took that woman into your house, Satan himself entered with her. She is a convicted witch, already under sentence of death for murder and divers other horrible crimes."

They were all staring at him. Darrell and Giles; the preacher; Barnaby. Staring in horror, and something of disbelief, Darrell said with difficulty:

"Are you certain of this?"

"Quite certain. I was present at her trial, and though she was not then named Rebecca Moone, there can be no doubt this is the same woman. It was in Essex, three years ago. A village there was grievously beset by witchcraft, even as your village, sir, has lately been, and when at length, by the mercy of God, the evil was unmasked, a whole witch-coven was discovered, of which this woman was the self-confessed leader. They were all found guilty and condemned to death, but because one of those whom Rebecca had killed was her own husband, she was judged guilty of petty treason and sentenced to die by fire instead of by the rope. Her followers were hanged, but Rebecca escaped."

"How, in God's name?"

"Say 'in the Devil's name,' Sir Darrell, and you will

come nearer the mark, for only he and the woman herself could tell you. On the eve of her execution she vanished from the cell in which she was confined, and it is commonly supposed that Satan himself snatched her thence. As well he may have done, for never, before or since, have I encountered a mortal being so thoroughly steeped in evil."

"The Devil may have delivered her from prison," Giles remarked absently, "but he had little care of her afterwards, to let her reach the pass in which Sir Darrell and his lady found her." He picked up Imelda's letter from the table where Darrell had let it fall, read it again, his face grim with anxiety, and then stowed it carefully away. He turned to Dr. Malperne, and suddenly he was brisk again. "Well, sir, are you satisfied? Will you go with us to Conyngton St. John, so that you may be present when the true source of all its present ills is challenged and made prisoner? You are very welcome, but I give you warning that we shall ride at first light."

"No." It was Tobias Swinlake who spoke, before the preacher could reply. There was deep trouble in his face and voice. "We dare not delay so long, but must ride now, as soon as we can get to horse, for tonight is August Eve, the eve of Lammastide. Tonight, beyond all doubt, the witches of Conyngton will gather to pay homage to their master, the Devil."

They rode out from Plymouth in the last afterglow of sunset and the light of a rising moon. Giles and Sir Darrell led the way, riding knee to knee, and Giles at least had a thought to spare for the irony of it, that he, the Cromwellian officer, the shipbuilder's son, should ride like a comrade beside a staunch Royalist of proud and ancient family. Yet comrades they were this night, bound by a common cause, each prepared to do battle with the powers of Hell for the woman he loved, Charity Conyngton in prison, Imelda at the Dower House, where dwelt also Rebecca Moone, the woman "thoroughly steeped in evil." If Rebecca learned that Imelda had discovered her—Giles's heart turned cold at the thought.

Behind him and Sir Darrell came Mr. Swinlake and the preacher, and they were followed by a sergeant and a score of red-coated troopers. They rode at a brisk trot, rending the stillness of the summer night with the rhythm of hoof-beats and rattle of accoutrements, while the last light faded from the sky behind them and the moon rose higher, changing slowly from a broad disc of palest gold into an orb of brilliant silver, flooding the countryside with its pale light. It was close on midnight when they reached Conyngton St. John, clattering and jingling through the sleeping village that looked deceptively peaceful under the moon, and breasting the long hill towards the Dower House and the ruins of the manor.

Their first intimation of something wrong came when they emerged from the belt of woodland into the park, and saw the windows of the house lighted and the front door standing open, spilling candlelight down the steps and on to the forecourt. Simultaneously, and without a word spoken, Giles and Darrell set spur to their mounts and dashed forward along the track as though competing in a race, with their startled companions, and the soldiers, careering after them.

The noise brought servants to the lighted doorway, and then a woman pushed her way between them and Giles knew one heady instant of relief before he saw that it was not Imelda. This woman was shorter, with auburn hair which in the candlelight glowed like copper. Roxanne!

"Darrell—and Major Bradwell!" she exclaimed, running down the steps as they flung themselves from their saddles. "Oh, thank God that you have come!" She held out her hands to Darrell, but her next words were for Giles. "Imelda is missing."

For the space of a heartbeat, the whole world was frozen for him in a pattern of silver and gold, moonlight and candle-glow, against a darkness which was suddenly colder and blacker than the darkness of a summer night. From a great way off he heard his own voice speaking.

"How long since?"

"She was seen walking through the orchard a little while before sunset, but her absence was not noticed until a couple of hours ago. The servants searched the house and garden, and then the bailiff came to inquire of me. I sent to the village, but there had been no sign of her there."

Darrell said sharply: "Where is Rebecca Moone?"

"Rebecca?" Roxanne sounded startled. "I do not know. She was here—I think—when I arrived, but—!"

She broke off, for he was already turning away to fire curt questions at the servants; questions which were repeated and passed to and fro among them until, a few minutes later, the answer came. Rebecca, too, was missing, and with her another woman, an ill-favoured wench who worked as scullery-maid.

"Not one witch in your household, Sir Darrell, but two," Mr. Swinlake said in a low voice. "There can be no doubt what hellish rendezvous they are keeping."

By this time they were in the hall, the four men and Roxanne, clustered together before the empty fireplace, and Darrell, in a few quiet words, had introduced Swinlake and explained the reason for their arrival. Roxanne stared at him in horror.

"And Imelda had found out? Heaven have mercy! Do you suppose Rebecca knew?"

"What else can we suppose?" Giles was in command of himself again, and his voice gave no hint of the agony clawing at him; at the fear, and the fury at his own helplessness. Where was she? What was happening to her while he stood here, not knowing how to bring her aid? "She would not be abroad until this hour of her own free will. She knows the danger of venturing beyond the immediate vicinity of the house, for I warned her of it the last time I was here."

"And she heeded the warning," Roxanne said wretchedly. "Except to church, she has not once been beyond the bounds of the garden and the orchard, not even to visit me."

Dr. Malperne spoke for the first time. "Parlous though Miss Hallett's plight may be, it cannot be our only concern. We came here to seize the witch, Rebecca Moone, and her companions in evil. To challenge the powers of Hell and free this place from the dominion of the foul Fiend. In the name of the Lord, I charge you, let us be about it with no more delay."

Giles turned on him with uncontrollable, barely suppressed fury, but Mr. Swinlake intervened, saying quickly:

"The Doctor is right, and both goals may well be reached by the same road. Find the one, and it is more than probable that we shall find the other."

"Find them? Aye, but how?" Giles's voice was rough with anxiety. "You, sir, know more of these matters than any of us. Where will these Devil-begotten hags meet?"

"I have been giving thought to that. Not at the church, though churchyards are often the meeting place of witches, for I marked this one as we rode hither, and it stands in the midst of the village. It must be some secret place, where none may witness their foul rites. Deep in the woods, maybe, or—" He paused. "What are the ruins I saw on the crest of the hill behind this house?"

"Conyngton?" Darrell exclaimed angrily. "They would not dare!" Then, rebuking himself: "And yet, why not? The village people shun the place, accounting it haunted."

"We will search there first." Abruptly Giles was in command again, issuing orders with no thought that they might be argued with or disobeyed. He strode to the door. "Sergeant, your men to horse! Sir Darrell guides us, and we go silently, with no word spoken henceforth. Mr. Swinlake, Dr. Halperne, you will be mindful of that command, if you please. Follow close behind Sir Darrell and me, as before."

Swept by that brisk authority, they went, Darrell with a little nod of grim approval at the ruthless efficiency of this Cromwellian officer. In a matter of moments, it seemed, the whole company had gone, melting quietly into the black and silver spaces of the neglected park, and Roxanne and the servants were left to a period of desperate anxiety and fearful speculation.

Circling the garden and orchard of the Dower House, Darrell led the way at a walk diagonally up the slope of the hill towards the manor, through moonlight and shadow beneath the scattered trees, and the troop followed with only the occasional snort of a horse or faint jingle of a bridle to betray its presence. They were approaching the wall surrounding the gardens when suddenly there came from somewhere beyond it, shocking in its incongruity, the lively lilt of a pipe.

Instinctively they drew rein, Giles flinging up his hand to halt the riders behind them, and for a moment or two they all sat, shaken and unbelieving, listening to the merry tune echoing weirdly amidst ruin and desolation. Giles said in a murmur of hushed exultation:

"By Heaven, we have them! We will go forward on foot—'tis quieter so. Where best to leave the horses?"

"There is a clump of oak trees yonder that will conceal them. Follow me."

Giles waved the troop forward again, and a few minutes later all were dismounted; the horses tethered and one of the troopers left to guard them. Then forward again, in the same order as before, to the foot of the wall and then to skirt it towards the gatehouse.

The piping had ceased, but as they approached the black mouth of the gateway, a woman's voice could be heard speaking not far away, although they could not make out the words. Then Darrell and Giles had reached the opening, and were looking through the black vault of the archway at a scene which was the very stuff of nightmare. Amid a reeking, sulphurous haze the witches knelt in homage before their horned deity, while at the creature's feet a little group was poised as though for some dark ritual. A suppliant, kneeling woman with two attendants, and Rebecca Moone stooping above her to offer instruction or command. Was this in fact an initiation? Were they witnessing the actual sealing of a pact with Satan?

Giles's flesh crawled with horror at the thought, and then Rebecca moved swiftly, the suppliant's head was jerked roughly up, and horror of another kind swept over him as he saw this was Imelda. In an instant of blinding clarity he realized what was about to happen, and with a shout he leapt forward through the archway, dragging out his sword as he went. As though shot from a sling he projected himself across the courtyard, and behind him came Darrell Conyngton and, behind Darrell, the disciplined troopers of the Ironside army.

The witches scattered, shrieking with alarm, but the shock of the interruption held the group on the steps motionless for the few seconds needed for Giles to reach them. Imelda was helpless, with Rebecca's fingers still twined in her hair, and the witch-god's dagger poised above her bare, defenceless throat. Giles's sword

gleamed blue-white in the moonlight as it swept in a
great arc and descended on the creature's upraised
arm with a strength that sheared through flesh and
splintered bone, and with a high-pitched scream of
agony, a scream that was wholly human, the beast-
headed monstrosity pitched forward down the steps.
The cunningly wrought goat mask was dislodged by
the fall and rolled aside, revealing the gaunt, livid
features of Daniel Stotewood.

Even as the mock Devil fell, Giles was stooping
above Imelda, sweeping her up into his arms and
springing on to the steps. Darrell, dashing after him,
checked for a moment in stupefaction as he realized
the identity of the witches' leader, and then concern
for his cousin took him to Giles's side.

Giles, clasping Imelda in his left arm, and with his
right hand still gripping the reddened sword, was glad
of Darrell's help to loosen the bonds about her wrists,
and they were both too intent upon the rescued girl
to be aware of the dark, shadowy form which stole
swiftly past them up the steps and drifted through
the doorway to disappear into the darkness of the
ruined hall.

A moment later their attention was drawn again to
the foot of the steps, where Stotewood, with blood
pouring from his almost severed arm, was somehow
dragging himself to his feet. Another cry rang out,
a terrible sound of mingled disbelief and fury and
shame, and Matty Weddon stumbled forward to fling
herself upon him, bearing him down again as she
stabbed and hacked at him with the dagger she had
snatched up from the ground. One of the troopers

sprang forward to restrain her, but she fought him with the strength of madness, and two of his comrades had to go to his aid before she could be subdued.

The rest of the coven had easily been made prisoner. Taken utterly by surprise, they had tried to escape, but Giles and Sir Darrell held the steps, and the soldiers had deployed to left and right as they emerged from the archway, into a line which in a matter of moments had encircled the forecourt, herding the frantic women together in its midst.

Imelda was barely conscious. The ordeal she had undergone, believing that she was at the mercy of the Devil incarnate, was a horror beside which even the imminence of death had seemed insignificant, and now she was only dimly aware that the ordeal was over. Slowly, painfully, she became conscious of certain things. Her arms had been unbound, and someone was gently chafing her numbed hands. She was half lying, half sitting on the ground, and someone else was holding her. The supporting arm was strong and warm and comforting, yet her cheek rested against an unyielding surface which was smooth and cool. Puzzled, she opened her eyes, then hurriedly closed them against the glitter of moonlight on polished steel. Steel? Steel and scarlet. Giles!

She opened her eyes again, and saw that it was indeed Giles who held her. Sir Darrell was there, too— it was he who was chafing her hands—but this did not seem to matter. She spoke Giles's name in a broken whisper, and gasped, and burst into tears.

His arms tightened about her for a moment, his hand moved gently, reassuringly, over her hair, and then he was rising to his feet, making her rise with him but still holding her, so that even when they stood upright she was still supported in his arms. He said quietly to Darrell:

"Best take her home. She has endured too much, and needs a woman's care."

Before Darrell could agree, Tobias Swinlake came hurrying up the steps. He looked both angry and disturbed.

"We have accomplished only part of our purpose. The woman Rebecca is not among those made prisoner."

"What?" Darrell was incredulous. "She was here, at the foot of the steps when we entered."

"And she did not pass through the archway, that I can swear, for Dr. Malperne and I were there the whole while. But she is not here now."

Imelda, hearing this, shuddered and cowered closer to Giles; the three men exchanged uneasy glances, remembering how once before the witch had escaped from what seemed certain captivity; Dr. Malperne, joining them as Swinlake spoke, shook his head in grim warning.

"Mark me, my friends, the powers of Hell are not yet vanquished here, for Satan has preserved the most favoured of his servants, spirited her away from the just anger of the godly, even as he preserved her once from the consuming fire. They worshipped a false Devil here, but the true Prince of Evil was not far away."

Giles, feeling Imelda trembling in his arms, was strongly tempted to thrust the preacher's warning back down his throat, and yet what other explanation was there? Rebecca Moone had certainly been here, for both he and Sir Darrell had seen her. Only a minute or two had passed from the moment he launched the attack until the witches were surrounded and captured, yet in that brief space of time Rebecca had disappeared.

For once he felt uncertain what to do. One part of his mind was wholly concerned with Imelda, with the need to get her away from this desolate, ill-omened place to her home, where she would be safe and cared for. Yet would she be safe, even there? Would any of them be safe as long as the witch-woman was at large, filled with vengeful fury at the destruction of her coven?

He could sense the uneasiness of his men as realization spread among them that the most dangerous of their quarry had evaded them. They were well disciplined, like all the New Model Army, but they were all, in their various independent ways, deeply religious, and the necessity was obviously to get them and their prisoners away from the grim scene of the witches' rites.

"Sergeant, bring up the horses," he said briskly. "Mount each prisoner behind one of the men, with another trooper to ride alongside. Then back to the Dower House while I take order how best to capture the woman who evaded us."

Plainly relieved, the sergeant went smartly about it, setting half a dozen troopers to guard the prisoners and drive them through the archway into the park, and the rest to fetch the horses. Leaving him to it, Giles picked Imelda up and strode down the steps and across the forecourt, neither knowing nor caring what Sir Darrell Conyngton thought of this high-handed carrying off of his kinswoman, and not waiting to see whether or not he and the other two men followed.

He was just emerging from the archway when a commotion arose from the direction of the trees where they had concealed their mounts. The snorting and whinnying of terrified horses, a man's voice shouting in mingled anger and fear, and then the drumming of hooves. Clearly visible in the brilliant moonlight, a rider shot from the direction of the trees and headed at a mad gallop across the hillside, away from the manor; a female figure, but riding astride like a man; bare-headed, with grey hair streaming behind her; Rebecca Moone.

As she passed out of sight, Giles found Sir Darrell at his side. "If we would take her at all, we must follow fast. There is only one way open to her in that direction—a track that leads straight up into the Moor."

"The Moor?" For a moment Giles's heart misgave him, for to follow a proven witch at midnight into the haunted expanse of Dartmoor was a prospect to make the boldest spirit pause. Then he realized that the other man had left him, was already racing towards the oak trees where the horses were, and he hesitated no longer. Tobias Swinlake and the preacher had joined him now, and to them he said quickly:

"Take Miss Hallett home. Mrs. Pennan will look after her." He raised his voice. "Sergeant! To the Dower House. Await me there."

He set Imelda on her feet, but she clung to him,

sobbing again, imploring him not to go.

"I must, love. She must be taken, and I cannot let Conyngton pursue her alone." He kissed her swiftly, careless of the onlookers, and then freed himself firmly from her clasp and followed Darrell.

Even before he reached the oak trees he saw the other man galloping away in the direction taken by Rebecca Moone, and a couple of minutes later was himself in the saddle and spurring in pursuit. He was just in time to see Sir Darrell leave the park through a broken gateway, and, following, found himself in a narrow lane between high banks where he had no choice but to check his headlong pace. Making what haste he could, he presently caught up with the squire, who had halted to wait for him.

"Follow me closely, Major," Darrell said briefly. "This is a treacherous road when one knows it not, and for the next mile or so we shall do better to make haste slowly."

Treacherous it certainly was, and yet Rebecca Moone had traversed it without mishap, for they found no trace of her until they emerged into more open country and saw the great rampart of the Moor towering before them. Even then, the only indication that their quarry was still ahead of them was a little cloud of dust on the crest of a rise a quarter of a mile away. They followed as quickly as they could without taking undue risks, for the surface of the lane was pitted with ruts and potholes, but now they were leaving the cultivated land behind them, the country through which they rode was becoming wilder of aspect, until at last the lane became a track winding between slopes carpeted with heather and they had reached the Moor itself.

Wild and mysterious, it stretched for miles on either hand beneath the moon, bog and heather and granite tor, a vast wilderness into which a fugitive might vanish without trace, but now the quarry was clear in view, the going was better and the more expert horsemanship of the pursuers began to tell. They were gaining on her, Giles's chestnut stallion half a length ahead of Sir Darrell's bay, when the stolen horse stumbled and went down, flinging its rider from the saddle into the heather.

She rolled over and over, but managed to regain her feet, only to see her mount, which had also scrambled up, bolting back the way it had come. For a second or two she stood staring after it, and at the two approaching riders, and then threw up her arms in a menacing and malevolent gesture and plunged off through the heather, away from the track. Giles heard Darrell call out something, but he had increased his lead by this time, intent upon a capture which now seemed imminent, and paid no heed.

It was a weird and desolate spot. To the right, a granite crag of odd and tortuous shape reared up above the heather, and beyond it the ground fell sharply to a hollow where trails of mist drifted and eddied like ghosts in the moonlight. Rebecca was fleeing down the slope, running desperately, and hoping, no doubt, that in such a place the riders would hesitate to follow, but Giles had no intention of allowing her to escape. He slackened speed, steadied his mount, and then urged it off the track into the heather.

A yard or two down the slope the stallion jibbed, snorting in terror, with ears laid back and rolling eyes. Giles, furious at the delay, for Rebecca was already out of sight, tried to force it on, and then, behind him, Darrell shouted again.

"Bradwell, wait! In God's name, hold back!"

There was such compelling urgency in his voice that Giles obeyed, only saying angrily over his shoulder:

"If we lose sight of her in this wilderness, we shall never find her. Would you let the hell-hag escape?"

"She will not. There is no escape for her that way."

Even as he spoke, a scream rang out somewhere nearby, a cry of such terror and despair that Giles's blood ran cold. It was the scream of one in the grip of an unimaginable doom; of a monster which, having once seized its prey, would not yield it up that side of Hell.

"The Lord defend us!" he said in an awed whisper. "What is it? What ails her?"

"Hagstone Mire," Darrell replied grimly. "We are upon the very brink of it. Go forward if you will, but dismounted, and one cautious pace at a time."

He swung out of the saddle as he spoke, and Giles followed his example. Very carefully, leading their reluctant horses, they edged their way forward past the crag to the spot where Rebecca had disappeared. Here the slope grew rapidly steeper, and a moment later they saw her below them, writhing and struggling frantically in the grip of the bog, into which she had already sunk above the knees. When she caught sight of them she screamed again, stretching out desperate arms, but she was beyond their reach, and even if they had had the will to save her, they had not the means.

She realized it as soon as they, and her screams for help became curses, the pleading hands were transformed into malevolent claws as she raved at them like one possessed; raved until the hatred and venom in her voice were overwhelmed by fear, by an awful terror of something more than death; and all the while the greedy black ooze was sucking her down and down. Sickened by the sight, they turned away and dragged and scrambled their way back to the safety of the track, but the dreadful screaming, hoarse now as a raven's call, still pursued them.

"Legend has it that the Mire is bottomless," Darrell said in a shaken voice. "Certainly it has never been known to give up its prey."

Giles took off his helmet and mopped his brow. He had seen death in many violent and dreadful forms, but there was a horror about this passing which he knew he would never forget.

"Did the Devil she pledged herself to save her from the fire only to cast her into the Pit?" he asked with a shudder. "Truly he is the very Prince of Lies."

The hoarse screaming was suddenly cut off by a choking gurgle more horrible than anything which had preceded it, and then a silence which seemed to contain a tangible quality of evil descended again over the eerie, savage landscape of Dartmoor. Giles and

Sir Darrell looked at each other, and mounted their horses, and rode together back to Conyngton.

A week had gone by, and Imelda was walking again in the orchard, though now it was not evening, but noontide. A fresh and lovely summer day, the hot sunshine tempered by a gentle breeze, the sky a deep and peaceful blue, for on the night after the witches' sabbath the thunderous heat had broken in a violent storm. Then, after two days of grey skies and intermittent rain, the clouds had cleared and the sun shone forth again on a world refreshed and cleansed. To Imelda there had been something symbolic in that, as though the elements themselves were reflecting the changes which had taken place.

For the witches were gone from Conyngton. With the death of Rebecca Moone, and of their false Devil— Daniel Stotewood had died there in the manor ruins, at the hands of the girl he had deceived and shamed— and the capture of the rest of the coven, the shadow of the powers of darkness had been lifted from the village. Sorrow there still was, for the witches had all been women of the parish. Charity's scullery-maid; four others, besides Matty, from the village itself and the surrounding farms; no less than five among the servants at the Moat House, including she who had been the children's nurse. They would never return. In Plymouth the law would take its course and they pay the penalty for their crimes, but these were the guilty, with the blood of an innocent child on their hands, and perhaps of one other, too, for Weddon the smith was dead. At the very time when his daughter was kneeling in homage to Satan, he had suffered another attack and this one had killed him. No one in Conyngton doubted that the coven had brought it about.

The guilty would suffer, but the innocent, the falsely accused, had been delivered from danger, and today Sir Darrell would bring his wife home. The Dower House had been in a fever of preparation since dawn, but now all was in readiness and Imelda had leisure to turn her thoughts to her own concerns. That these should take a gloomy direction was inevitable, for she had neither seen nor heard from Giles since he left her to pursue the fleeing Rebecca Moone.

Why had he not come, or sent any word? He must know that once Sir Darrell returned to Conyngton they would have no opportunity to meet, for though the squire would undoubtedly recognize the need which had caused Imelda to disobey him while Charity was in danger, it was too much to hope that he would be equally complaisant now.

She came to the stile and looked across it up the hill to the crumbling wall and the ruins glimpsed beyond. A shiver shook her, in spite of the warmth of the day, induced partly by the memory of the horror she had faced there, and partly because the shattered shell of the mansion was a visible reminder of everything that stood between her and the man she loved. She sighed, turning to walk back down the gentle slope towards the house, then checked at sight of the flash of scarlet and glint of steel moving towards her beneath the branches laden with ripening fruit.

Next moment she was running, stumbling in the

long orchard grass, to be caught in an embrace which swept her clear off her feet and deprived her of breath. She clung joyfully to him until at last he set her down, holding her before him to look searchingly into her face.

"You are well?" he asked anxiously. "Wholly recovered?"

"Very well—now!" She spoke without shyness, looking up at him with shining eyes. "Oh, Giles, I have longed for you to come!" Then sudden recollection clouded her eyes. "But today of all days! Sir Darrell and her ladyship are expected. They may arrive at any moment."

"I know." Just for an instant the shadow of an earlier sternness was in his face and his voice. "Did you suppose I would come creeping to you behind Conyngton's back, now that all peril is past?"

"Is it past?" For the moment she allowed herself to ignore the first part of his question. "Is there really no more to fear?"

"Nothing more. The confessions of those we took prisoner have wholly exonerated Lady Conyngton, and she is now seen to be as much a victim as her aunt. Who, so I am told, begins to recover." With an arm about her sholders, he led her to a corner of the orchard where one of the big old apple trees, long since fallen, had been left to provide a low, mossy seat. "This whole parish owes its deliverance to you."

She shook her head. "To you also, Giles, for had not Mr. Swinlake come here at your behest, no one would ever have known who Rebecca really was."

"No one knows it now," he told her ruefully, "even

in the place where she was first condemned as a witch, for she came there, none knew whither."

Imelda was frowning. "Is it known how Daniel Stotewood came into the matter?"

"No, nor ever will be, since only Rebecca Moone knew who he was. To the rest, he was the god they worshipped, the Devil made flesh, whom Rebecca claimed to have called forth from Hell by her magical powers." He paused, seriously regarding her. "Imelda, why did you follow her to the manor that evening? You knew that I would come as soon as I received your message, and your suspicions alone would have been sufficient warranty for her arrest. When we arrived here at midnight, and learned that you could not be found—!" He stopped abruptly, his hand tightening painfully upon hers. "I knew fear then such as I had never known before, and pray never to know again."

Imelda hesitated for no more than a moment. "I did not follow her, Giles. I lied when Mr. Swinlake questioned me, but I cannot lie to you." Hurriedly she described the errand which had taken her to the manor ruins. "Forgive me. I should not have disregarded your warning to stay within the garden."

"I was not reproaching you, sweetheart," he said quickly. "You are right. Had those things been found, it might well be that her ladyship would not be riding home today." He paused, still clasping her hand, his steady gaze holding hers. "They will be here soon, and it is time now to turn our thoughts to our own concerns. I have come for your answer, Imelda. Will you marry me?"

Her eyes filled with tears. "Sir Darrell and my father will never give consent."

"Then we will marry without it, but, my love, you must be very sure. Can you endure complete estrangement from your family and friends, your Church, and the loyalties in which you have been reared? Can you embrace my way of life, my faith? These are questions you must ask yourself, and answer, before you answer mine."

Gently she withdrew her hand from his, and reached up to lift the helmet from his head and lay it in the grass at their feet. Then she took his face between her hands and looked into his eyes.

"They were answered long since," she said softly. "I can endure anything, my dear love, except to be parted from you. Yes, I will marry you."

They lingered in the orchard until the sound of approaching horses warned them that the Conyngtons were arriving, and then they hurried back to the house so that Imelda could be at the door to greet them. Every servant in the house had crowded into the hall, while grooms and gardeners gathered outside, and Giles remained quietly in the background, knowing that this was a moment in which he had no part.

He watched Imelda run down the steps as the horses halted at their foot, and then after a little while she and Charity came in together. Charity's arm was about Imelda's waist, her free hand extended towards the servants pressing forward to welcome her. For a minute or two she was completely surrounded, and it was left to her husband, following her into the house, to notice the tall, steel-and-scarlet figure on the far side of the hall.

"Bradwell!" he exclaimed in surprise, and some annoyance. "I did not look to see you here!"

"Major Bradwell?" Charity looked quickly round, and then gently disengaged herself from the servants and went forward with outstretched hand. "I am so glad to see you, Major, and to have an opportunity of thanking you. I owe you a debt which can never be repaid."

He had been standing stiffly with his helmet held in the crook of his arm, looking with faintly challenging eyes at Sir Darrell, but now he took Charity's hand, and bowed, saying with a slight smile:

"If I looked for payment, my lady, I have it now, in witnessing your homecoming. Believe me, I am as happy as any here to see you safely restored to your family."

"Which I would not have been, sir, without your aid," she replied seriously. "Come, let us go in. You will stay to dine with us, will you not?" She cast a smiling glance over her shoulder. "Imelda?"

They followed her and Sir Darrell into the parlour, and while one of the servants poured wine, Imelda said to Charity:

"The children are in the nursery, cousin. I thought you would prefer to greet them privately."

She had been unfastening from her waist the silver chain which held the household keys, and now she brought them to Charity and put them into her hand. "I have governed all to the best of my ability, cousin, but I never have been more glad to restore a charge to one whose right it is. The Dower House has been a sad place without its mistress."

"My dear!" Charity, taking the keys, took also the hand that proffered them, and pressed it warmly between her own. Imelda returned the clasp, but then withdrew her fingers and moved to stand beside Giles. Charity looked at them both, and there was sudden comprehension in her eyes. A trust had been justified, and a duty discharged.

She dismissed the servant, and, when the door had closed behind him, looked at her husband. He was watching her, but she knew with loving certainty that he was thinking only of the fact that they were together again in their own home, with her danger past and their most pressing anxieties relieved. He was not thinking of Imelda and Giles, except with slight impatience that they were there at all, but unless she was much mistaken he would be obliged to think of them before long, for it was certainly not chance which had brought Major Bradwell to the Dower House that day. Her glance passed on and came to rest, faintly questioning, on the young man's face.

Giles set down, untasted, his glass of wine, and turned to the squire. "Sir Darrell," he said quietly, "now that her ladyship is, happily, delivered from danger, I am at liberty to tell you that your kinswoman, Miss Hallett, has honoured me by consenting to become my wife."

Darrell stared at him, so taken aback that for the moment he was, quite literally, bereft of words, and even Charity gasped. This was plain dealing, indeed. No humble seeking of Darrell's consent, or of his help in approaching Imelda's father; just a simple statement of fact, spoken with perfect courtesy yet in a tone which recognized no possibility of denial; though, of course, denial would come.

Come it did. "So Miss Hallett has consented?" Darrell said at length, angrily sarcastic. "If it is the custom, Major, among those of your persuasion, for a young woman to dispose of her hand without the consent, or even the knowledge of her family, it is not so among ours. Miss Hallett will marry, if marry she does, a husband of her family's choosing."

"I fear, Sir Darrell," Giles said quietly, "that I have not made my meaning plain. Miss Hallett is to be my wife. For her sake, I hope it will be with your consent, so that she will not be completely estranged from her family, but if you withhold that consent— why then, I shall regret it, but I shall still marry her."

There was a brief, tense pause. Darrell was staring at Giles as though he could not believe what the Major had said—as he probably could not, Charity reflected wryly. In a moment or two, disbelief would again be overtaken by anger, but she could see that even the fiery Conyngton temper would have no more effect on the unshakable determination of the young soldier than the sea breaking against a rock. To bridge the dangerous silence she asked reasonably:

"What of your own family, Major Bradwell? Is it not possible that they will dislike such a match as greatly as my husband does?"

A quick, searching glance from the blue-grey eyes acknowledged the fact that she had not coupled herself with Darrell in that dislike. He said courteously:

"My lady, it is my hope—indeed, my belief—that they will accept my bride. If they do not," he shrugged, "I am my own master, and concede to no man the right to tell me who I may or may not marry. In either event, you need have no fear that my wife will not be well provided for."

Charity nodded as though satisfied, but Darrell struck the table with his fist, exclaiming angrily: "Enough of this folly! Bradwell, I am well aware of the debt I owe you, but when my cousin Hallett placed his daughter in my care he delegated to me the responsibility for her future, and I would betray his trust if I consented to a marriage of which neither he nor I can approve."

Giles looked at him for a moment; then he made a little gesture of resignation. "So be it. I am sorry." He turned to Imelda. "We will go to Plymouth. My Colonel's wife will extend you her protection until we can be married. Will you come with me, Imelda?"

Her eyes were wide, startled. "Now?"

He nodded. "Now. There is no more to be said, and since the parting must come, better that it come swiftly." He laid his hands on her shoulders, turning her more fully to face him. "But remember, my love, there can be no turning back."

"I know." Her eyes, lifted towards him, were unclouded by doubt or hesitation, peaceful with certainty. "I will go with you, Giles, wheresoever you will, now and always."

"I forbid it!" Darrell's voice was unsteady with anger, and with disbelief. "I forbid you to leave this house. In God's name, girl, what madness possesses you? Have you no conscience? Will you deny the faith in which you have been reared, the Cause for which your brothers fought and died?"

"Yes," she replied faintly. She was deathly pale, clinging tightly to Giles's hand for comfort and support, but unshakable in her determination. "I do not want to quarrel with you, or seem ungrateful to you and Cousin Charity but I cannot obey you. I can only pray that one day you will be able to forgive me."

He stared at her in angry bafflement. Short of wresting her by force from her lover—a course as undignified as it was unlikely to succeed—he could not prevent her departure; and if she left now with Bradwell, there could be no question of later hindering their marriage. It was not that Darrell distrusted Giles Bradwell. He respected, and even liked, the young man enough to regret that they were upon opposing sides, but to be defied in his own house by a slip of a girl who owed him obedience; to stand tamely aside and let her depart with an enemy, with a man he had already forbidden to her—this was something which his pride would not let him accept.

It was Charity who understood and resolved his dilemma. She had long foreseen this situation, although she had not expected it to develop so openly and so soon, and because she understood her husband better than he understood himself, she saw now the need to provide him with the means to retreat in good order, to accept the inevitable with no sacrifice of pride or dignity. She moved forward to stand beside him.

"Darrell," she said gently, "can we not be generous?

We have so much this day for which to be thankful, and we owe a vast debt of gratitude to Imelda and to Major Bradwell, for it is they who gave us back each other. I beg of you, give your consent to their marriage."

He looked at her, frowning. "In payment of our debt to them?"

"No." She smiled and shook her head. "Because *I* ask it of you." She laid her hand on his arm. "My dear, do you not understand? You cannot part them from each other, any more than Jonas was able to part me from you."

There was a pause, while she willed him silently to agree, and Imelda waited with breathless anxiety. At last Darrell laid his hand over his wife's and looked at Imelda and Giles.

"Because my lady asks it of me," he said heavily, "and because on this of all days I can deny her nothing, I will do as she wishes. I cannot pretend to like this marriage, but I will place no obstacles in your path, and undertake to see that my cousin Hallett does not, either. You need not take my kinswoman from my house, Bradwell, until she leaves it as your bride."

Silently Giles bowed his agreement and his thanks, and Imelda, with a gasp of joyous relief, cast herself in Charity's arms. The older woman embraced her warmly, smiling above her head at Giles, but then put her gently aside and turned to Darrell.

"Let us go up to the nursery," she said to him. "I can wait no longer to see our children again."

She walked towards the door, and Giles went to open it for her, taking the opportunity to murmur his thanks. Sir Darrell started to follow, but was detained by Imelda, who caught his hand in hers and carried it swiftly to her lips.

"Thank you, cousin," she whispered. "You will never have cause to regret your generosity, I promise you."

"I hope not, my child," he replied seriously, "and I hope that you never have cause to regret it, either."

He went out. Giles closed the door and turned back to Imelda, holding out his arms, and she went into them like a homing bird.

"No doubts, my heart?" he asked softly. "No fears that your kinsman's misgivings may be justified?"

She shook her head, looking up at him with clear, untroubled eyes. How could there be doubts, when a miracle had been granted them; when from the horror and despair of a week ago they had been lifted into this transcendent blaze of happiness? To doubt would be a denial of faith itself.

"None, dear love," she replied tranquilly. "Come joy, come sorrow, I am content, so that we meet it together."